NORMAN CONQUEST 2066

David was dead from the moment of impact; his neck broken even before the car exploded into flames . . .

And miles away, on the other side of town, a young girl called his name, choking and writhing in an agony of fear . . .

Coincidence? ESP? Or just another piece of the jigsaw of mankind's evolution?

Also by J. T. McIntosh

THIS IS THE WAY THE WORLD BEGINS

and published by Corgi Books

J. T. McIntosh

Norman Conquest 2066

CORGI BOOKS
A DIVISION OF TRANSWORLD PUBLISHERS LTD

NORMAN CONQUEST 2066

A CORGI BOOK 0 552 10484 1

First publication in Great Britain

PRINTING HISTORY
Corgi edition published 1977

This book is set in 10/10½ pt Plantin

Corgi Books are published by Transworld Publishers Ltd.,
Century House, 61–63 Uxbridge Road,
Ealing, London, W.5.
Made and printed in Great Britain by
Hunt Barnard Printing Ltd., Aylesbury, Bucks.

Norman Conquest 2066

I

The worst, saddest ghost towns are boom towns that haven't made it.

Sherburn, built as a London overflow 'new town' around the turn of the century, with a brand-new motorway leading straight to it, had never made it. The broad, spacious, tree-lined London Road in the town center, the continuation of the freeway which ended officially on the outskirts, was a lavish stage setting for a play whose backers ran out of money before opening night.

It was an avenue of anomaly. Bright, freshly-painted shops glittered beside boarded-up ruins, neatly-curtained upstairs windows were flanked by peeling shutters, gleaming cars were parked outside shabby buildings, ancient buggies stood outside chrome-and-glass palaces.

At the far end of London Road, where one side started to be residential, two buildings which glowered at each other across the street told the sad story. The huge office block on the commercial side, designed to be an industrial executive powerhouse, was derelict. More than half of the huge windows were smashed, the rest so dirty they were opaque. The house of Meredith Dundee on the other side, set well back from the road, had well-kept gardens, an immaculate neo-Victorian exterior, and – if you could get through the gates and hedges and walls to the rear of the house and see it – a heated outdoor swimming pool which actually had water in it, sparkling blue-green water at that.

Meredith Dundee had come to terms with the world of 2066 A.D. The commercial palace had not.

Back in the busier parts of London Road the people maintained the inconsistent consistency. First, there were not nearly enough of them. Then there were men and women in rags and people in new suits, boys with no shoes and girls in smart calf-length black dresses, old women in shawls and youths in gear so sharp it hurt the eyes, children with dirty faces and children who shone.

From one of the cleanest-looking establishments in the street, a bakery, a gray rat darted. Nobody paid any particular attention, though several women watched it nervously and were clearly relieved when it disappeared into an empty house. One young housewife who had been about to enter the bakery changed her mind and went on to another shop a few doors away, a food shop which seemed remarkably well supplied with every form of food, among shops scantily stocked. Over the frontage a neon light which even in bright sunlight was working – the only one in the entire length of London Road – traced out the letters SALLY WELLS.

As the housewife went in, Sally Wells herself came out. Briefly she glanced back at the frontage to make sure that all was well – she visited the two shops at least once a day, at irregular times, not so much to catch the shopgirls on the hop as to ensure that it never came to that – and mounted the gleaming bicycle that was propped at the kerb, pulling away strongly without a wobble.

She was a pretty girl of nineteen, a blonde and a true blonde at that. Girls who dyed to be blondes generally went for bright gold, not Sally's sun-bleached yellow. She wore a powder-blue shorts suit, and that alone immediately set her apart. No other woman in the street wore bright blue, bright anything. And no other girl wore a particularly short skirt, far less brief, thin, clinging shorts.

This was only one of the most superficial ways in which Sally Wells was exceptional. She was the exception that proved the rule.

She turned right and then left in the nearly traffic-free streets and presently came to another shop, identical with the first, but in an even seedier street, Cornwall Place. She propped her bicycle against the kerb as before and strode in.

There were a dozen people in the shop, and the tall dark

girl behind the counter was becoming flustered. Without a word Sally joined her and helped out. She was quick and decisive and made her customers so. Instead of dithering as they were inclined to do with Arleen, who dithered too, they pulled themselves together in the face of Sally's briskness and made up their minds what they wanted. Within five minutes the shop was clear.

'That settles it,' Sally said briskly. 'You get an assistant.'

'I can manage,' said Arleen obstinately. It was an old subject.

'You weren't managing very well,' Sally retorted.

Arleen Jones brushed long dark hair from her eyes and said defensively: 'It's just Mr Wells not being here today – '

'Mr Wells hardly ever is here. Since he got me to put my name over the door instead of his he's retired, at the age of twenty-six. When do you ever see him now?'

She saw Arleen wince. It was a nuisance Arleen fancying herself in love with David – and, far worse, fancying David in love with her.

Arleen was not a pretty girl, but she could have made much more of herself. Taller and more opulent than Sally, who was the epitome of miniaturized nubility, she could have done far better than choose the too-tight dark sweaters and jeans she always wore, her sweaters crushing braless breasts which might have been magnificent and her overtightened belt giving her a protuberant belly she didn't possess.

And even then David wouldn't look at her twice. David wasn't emotionally stirred by anything but his car. He wasn't interested in the shops, leaving everything to Sally. She would not have minded except that getting food to sell was now becoming so much more difficult than selling it that she had to spend most of her time on that end of the business, with little time left for the shops, which were supposed to be David's responsibility.

It was a nuisance Arleen developing such a crush on David, because that meant she resolutely opposed other girls being employed in the shop. Sally didn't want to lose her because she was honest and reasonably efficient, if rather unstable, and if it were not for this new thing about David, Sally could put her in charge of the two shops, while she herself devoted more time to foraging.

If you had a food shop, let alone two, you had to go out and about visiting farms, mills, bakeries, factories, bullying the people there into promising supplies and then keep on bullying until they kept their promises. Fortunately David's preoccupation with his huge old estate car came in handy there. He didn't mind picking up goods once she had done the work of ensuring they were there.

'He'll be back today, though, won't he?' Arleen asked eagerly.

'Yes, and he'll have to come here if he's got anything. There isn't a deep-freeze at the other shop.'

'Fish, isn't it?'

'If he got any.' Sally had no inflated idea of her brother's business capacities.

On the point of pressing Sally further, trying to induce her to promise that David would be back soon and would spend the rest of the day at the store, Arleen suddenly gasped and pressed her hand to her heart.

'Indigestion?' Sally inquired without much sympathy. Sally was not sympathetic over the weakness of others.

'Where did David go?' said Arleen urgently. 'I mean, how is he coming back? Which road?'

'The motorway, I expect. The London Road. It's not the direct road, but he always uses it when – '

'David,' Arleen breathed. 'Be careful, David . . . '

Sally's eyes narrowed. She knew very well that Arleen had moments of foresight. Sally was rather impatient with such things, but it was impossible to deny facts, and the facts were that more than once Arleen had demonstrably known something was going to happen before it did . . .

David was seven miles away, on the motorway.

When Sally had asked him to go to Felixstowe, having heard rumors that substantial fish landings were being made somewhere in the area and a man on the spot with ready cash might secure a box or two, he had not been very keen until a friend wrote that he had discovered an old tire dump at Ipswich, and gave precise directions for finding it. Sally's commission then became an excellent excuse to take a day off and go to Ipswich. Felixstowe was only a few miles farther on.

Since he had turned onto the motorway a few miles back he had not seen a single vehicle. He was pleased to observe that nevertheless a half-hearted attempt had been made to repair the worst potholes in the road.

David was enjoying himself, as far as it could be said that he ever enjoyed himself. He was at the wheel of a car.

The motorway into Sherburn was one of the last major constructional projects to be carried through in England. Ironically, the 'new towns' like Sherburn, developed within seventy miles of London to relieve pressure on an overgrown capital, had never been really necessary, and therefore the motorway to Sherburn was even less necessary. For all the traffic that used it now an 18ft. two-way road would have been adequate. Such a road might have got more realistic maintenance, too.

Having discovered that the repairs had been done only on the middle lane, David drove at about sixty straight down the middle. His old Manson-Ford estate car was in better shape than most vehicles. Every time he found an abandoned Manson-Ford he cannibalized it, taking not only the parts he needed but also the parts he might eventually need.

He had no fish but he had got the tires. He felt rather guilty about this, because he had filled the rear of the car with so many tires that, big as it was, there was no room for fish. He had therefore not bothered to go on to Felixstowe at all. Naturally he had gone to the old dump first, and there, under surface garbage, quite a few reasonably sound tires of the right type survived. They had, of course, been discarded once as finished. Nevertheless, at least half a dozen of them were in better shape than the four on his car.

He was not going to lie to Sally. He'd tell her what had happened and she'd look exasperated but not surprised. She never was surprised when he made a mess of something, only on the few occasions when he managed to do something right. Well, he'd get the fish for her. Tomorrow or the next day or maybe next week.

Visibility was excellent and David saw the train when it was at least five miles away. Merely to see a train these days, a moving train, was an event. Although railway track was easier to maintain than a motorway, and the steam engines rescued from the scrapheap were virtually immortal, travel itself was ceasing to be worthwhile and only an occasional freight train ran. There would have been fewer still but for the fact that the Gardner factory in Sherburn was the only plant in the whole of Europe producing gasolene from coal, and the other sources were drying up.

It was interesting that the train and David's car were going to arrive at the level crossing virtually together.

There should never, of course, have been trains crossing a motorway on the same level. However, ten years ago when the railway bridge over the highway collapsed, it proved impossible to replace it. The steel, the labor and the money were equally unavailable. Besides, traffic on the road was negligible.

So the track was laid across the road. Otherwise Sherburn would have lost its rail link. And the rest of Britain would have lost Sherburn's gas, light oil and heavy oil – not only because trucks were more difficult to keep running than trains, but more important, because trucks, though they might have taken away the products, could not transport enough coal to keep the hydrogenation plant running.

In the event, the fact that trains occasionally crossed the road didn't make much difference. The motorway never had much traffic and there were few trains. Visibility in all directions was good. There was scarcely any more danger of collision than there was of two of the dozen or so airborne craft still operating in England colliding in mid-air.

David neither accelerated nor slowed. It was a momentary diversion that the only two fast-moving machines within five miles were attempting, by pure chance, to occupy the same space at the same time. As the last few hundred yards were eaten up by the car and the train, the coincidence of the paths of both became genuinely exciting.

David could still pull up and let the train go through. He could still accelerate and beat the train by a split second.

But that would beg the question, a question he now passionately wanted answered – *what would happen if he did nothing whatever about it?*

The Manson-Ford and the locomotive reached the crossing exactly simultaneously. The nose of the car and the nose of the engine completed a right-angle. The car was flung spinning back across the road and off it into waste land. The fuel tank exploded and the tires inside the car blazed instantly, fiercely. Oily black smoke boiled upwards.

David was dead from the moment of impact, his neck broken among seven other causes of death, even before there was time for him to be burned to death.

The heavy train scarcely felt the impact. The driver, alone in his cabin, first saw the car when it was windmilling crazily across the road and into the side. He gasped and reached for the controls.

Then his hands dropped. What could he do anyway? For ten minutes or more it would be impossible to get near the blazing car. Now the spare scrub was burning too, making a ring of fire round the swelling black smoke.

It would be better to go on into Sherburn and phone the fire department there.

This he did.

It didn't do any good. Nobody answered. The phone at the fire station was off the hook. It had been a bad day for fires. And it turned out to be a worse one.

'David,' Arleen whispered again.

'What about David?' said Sally impatiently.

'I don't know. It isn't clear.'

'Then shut up about him.' Sally had very little patience with anything she could not see, hear, smell, taste or touch. She had to admit that Arleen had a certain gift, but she wished Arleen would keep it to herself.

Arleen ran to the door, opened it and dashed outside. With an exclamation of annoyance Sally followed her. Arleen ran across the street, heedless of traffic. If the traffic in Cornwall Place had been what it was a century ago, she would never have reached the other side.

There was, however, no vehicular traffic except an old truck which had just passed, trailing clouds of blue smoke.

On the opposite side of the street, Arleen screamed: 'Look!' and pointed. Then she collapsed.

Rising above the buildings at the end of the street were clouds of thick black smoke. The fire must be miles away, out of town. What it could have to do with David Sally couldn't guess, but it worried her. Arleen had suddenly been struck with fear for David, had known where to look, and the smoke came from a place where David might very well be.

Sally bent over Arleen, who was writhing and choking, clutching not her heart but her middle. Sally released the too-tight belt, pulled out the tight sweater . . . and stared incredulously. But a middle-aged man and woman came to help, and she brushed the sweater back over Arleen's midriff.

Arleen stopped choking and sat up. Sally left her where she was, ran back across the road and jumped on her bicycle.

There were plenty of people to attend to Arleen. David, if he was involved in something that could send thick clouds of black smoke hundreds of feet in the air, was a far more pressing concern than Arleen.

As she pedalled madly towards the outskirts of town, she thought, however, not of David – because at the moment thinking about David, in the absence of information, was pointless – but about Arleen.

First she realized with surprise that she knew very little about Arleen, though the girl had worked for her for nearly a year. David had taken Arleen in his car two or three times, because every enthusiast wants to show off his pride and joy and talk about it. Apart from that Arleen had had no social contact with either of them.

Only now did Sally realize that she had never seen Arleen in the washroom, never seen her in anything but a sweater and trousers. Otherwise she would not have been surprised.

Arleen was covered with fur. Short, dark, fine fur. Round the navel was a smooth bare pale oval. Elsewhere, in the rib cavity, round the waist, on the abdomen, she was a furry animal.

Twice before Sally had encountered hairy people. They were both men, lustful men, and they had come at her in the dark. On both occasions she had made her escape without pausing to satisfy her curiosity.

She had not thought much about the hairiness of the men. Men could have hairy legs, hairy arms, hairy chests, shoulders, stomachs, even backs, without being freaks. Sally had no husband or lover, but she was no virgin. She had seen men naked.

She had also seen many women naked, for she played most games and took part in many other sporting activities. Unselfconscious herself, she automatically encouraged unselfconsciousness in others, and in many a dressing-room, locker-room, showerbath or steamroom she had seen women of all ages, shapes and sizes.

She had never seen a girl with hair like Arleen's. Now she knew that Arleen, who was not very attractive anyway, had another cross to bear. She was a freak.

Sally was fastidious about hair. She regularly expended time and trouble to ensure that the only hair on her entire body was on her head.

She reached the start of the motorway and pedalled on. It didn't matter any more which lane she took. There was nothing on either carriageway.

Sally assumed, and correctly, that she would reach the scene of the fire before anybody else. (The police, when they heard about the incident from the engine driver, asked questions. The ambulance service said that if the report was accurate there was no need for an ambulance. The fire service, finally contacted, said they'd be out as soon as they could – if nothing else, that gorse fire had to be stopped – but it might be a couple of hours before they could round up the men. If anybody came in, they'd send him out in a fire van to see what he could do.)

As it happened, the grass fire was out by the time Sally got there and threw herself off her bicycle, coughing as the smell of burning rubber caught her throat. The fire had failed to jump the track or the road, and a previous recent gorse fire had acted as a firebreak. But the car was still erupting like a volcano, though its twisted shape was quite unrecognizable.

Logic told her that the car was David's and that since the driver had not been thrown out and must still be in the car, David was dead.

Sally virtually knew the car was David's, yet she kept looking along the road for the familiar old Manson-Ford to appear.

Sally was different from most people.

She fought. She even fought the truth, fought to change it. Defeat was virtually unknown to her. This did not mean that victory came easy – far from it. She fought for it.

She would have fought her way to the car somehow, over the

still smoking grassland, through the choking smoke, if there had been the remotest chance of saving David. But although she was obstinate, she was no fool. Flames and smoke gushed from the windowless skeleton of what had been a car. There was no chance that anything remained alive in the wreck. The only chance was that it was not David's car.

It was not much of a chance. She could see what had happened – the car had hit a train. It had hit the train because David, proud of the car, proud of the work he had done on the car, had raced it. Or stubbornly refused to give way to the train (they had that in common, stubbornness, but David's was somehow ineffectual, always ending in defeat). Or even – and this had the ring of truth – leaving the whole thing to chance. *Heads I make it, tails I don't.*

Still she kept looking along the road . . . until she spotted something on the crossing – a small plastic doll that David had in the car as a mascot.

She stopped looking. Tears formed and ran down her face. She didn't sob. And presently the tears ceased. Too many people cried too easily.

She had lost a brother who, after all, had been lost all his life.

The woman almost rushed into the consulting room, desperation on her face, already saying: 'Doctor, I'm so glad you could see me . . . '

Then she stopped in dismay.

Anastasia merely cocked an inquiring eyebrow.

'I didn't know you were a woman,' the visitor said. 'Only that you were Dr Hersholt.'

'No need to use the past tense, Mrs Daley. I still am Dr Hersholt. I'd have thought you'd prefer a woman doctor. Most women do.'

'But you see, I'm not the patient. It's my son Beverley.'

'He's too ill to come himself?'

'No . . . not exactly. Though he never goes out. I can't get him to see a doctor, not even a man. I'll never get him to see you. Even if you called – '

'Then you'll have to tell me about it, won't you? Please sit down.'

The woman did so, uneasily, still staring at Anastasia.

Anastasia guessed at part of the trouble. Mrs Daley was perhaps the ugliest woman she had ever seen, short of injury or illness. There was nothing particularly wrong about the woman's face or body except that the items didn't match. There were large, watery eyes, a nose which managed to be both large and weak, a big, slack mouth. The amorphous body was more like that of a middle-aged man than a woman.

Anastasia, although she had long ceased admitting her age – since, in fact, she could no longer decently say 'Twenty-nine' – must, she hoped and believed, present a burning contrast. Women didn't like women doctors to be attractive. They liked the motherly type, and Anastasia was not motherly.

However, the woman plunged. She was not very coherent, but nevertheless Anastasia understood her very well, seeing through and behind the words.

Beverley Daley, it was clear, was the apple of his mum's eye. He was twenty-four and had grown from the prettiest baby into the most handsome young man . . . Anastasia, sifting the evidence, could not decide whether that meant he was really handsome or as ugly as his mother, for Mrs Daley would have said the same anyway. Other things she could be surer about. Mrs Daley's smothering love had prevented Beverley from growing up – it was a common pattern. His mother didn't want him to grow up, and neither did he, particularly. The matter of girls was simple enough. With such a mother and little contact with the outside world, Beverley had no great curiosity, no great desire to meet other members of the female sex. He literally didn't know what he was missing.

All this, however, seemed to have nothing directly to do with Beverley's current illness, which did appear to be a physical illness rather than one of the multitudinous psychosomatic disorders which usually came Anastasia's way. She believed the woman was trustworthy regarding Beverley's symptoms, which were:

First, loss of appetite and nausea, starting some two months ago. 'Of course, Beverley has always been sickly,' said Mrs Daley with some pride. A 100 per cent healthy youngster would have been no use to her, Anastasia thought. If he hadn't had the usual childhood illnesses for her to nurse him through, she would have trained him to have them.

Later, a dry mouth, cramp, an occasionally swollen tongue.

Then an uncontrollable itching. Beverley complained he couldn't wear nylon. Then wool. Then cotton. For some days he sat in the sun in the back garden, wearing only shorts. He said the itch was still hellish, but more bearable. And the cramp wasn't so bad.

What had driven Mrs Daley that day to search for a doctor, any doctor, was the fact that Beverley's mind had suddenly started wandering. He spoke of things which had happened years ago as if they were yesterday. He spoke of his father, whom he couldn't possibly remember, as being in the room.

'Did he speak of a girl?' Anastasia asked. After all, surely Beverley at least looked out of windows.

The woman's honest surprise was a better answer than her words. No, there had been no mention of any girl. So it wasn't that. Or if it was, it was repressed.

Anastasia temporized. She would have to see Beverley Daley before she could be sure. Yet an incredible picture was forming in her mind . . .

'How do *you* feel about women doctors?' she asked.

The woman's look of distrust, again not her words, gave the answer. Dr Anastasia Hersholt was not to come near her Beverley. 'We always used to go to Dr Smith,' Mrs Daley said obliquely. 'He was such a nice man, he said "Come and see me any time." He didn't often call, but he reassured me a lot . . . '

Anastasia got the picture. She knew of Smith, who had died six months ago. Indolent, old-fashioned, friendly, he had managed to convince himself in his last years that he was doing most good by sitting in his comfortable old chair and talking to people. He had not been anything but a talking doctor for years.

But Beverley's illness had nothing to do with Dr Smith or the death of Dr Smith. Anastasia could still scarcely believe her own conclusions, yet it was as plain as the nose on Mrs Daley's face.

'Wait here,' she said, getting up. 'I'll give you a prescription.'

'It'll cure Beverley?' said the woman eagerly.

'It'll help if he takes it. But you mustn't force him. Understand that, Mrs Daley – forcing him will be fatal.'

'Fatal?' said the woman, frightened.

'Sorry, I spoke loosely, a thing I seldom do. Forcing him will make him resist. Let him take it or not, as he likes. As much as he likes.'

She went into the adjoining dispensary and pondered a problem she had never had to face in all her long medical experience. Yet it was quite likely that now that it had happened she would encounter it again. The case of Beverley Daley, whom she was not allowed to see, was more important than Beverley Daley himself. What did a doctor do in circumstances which had probably never faced any doctor in human history before?

She thought of making up a bottle of green iron tonic, but that was too familiar and nobody would put much trust in a bottle of green tonic. Some outlandish color, magenta or turquoise? That might make a delicate stomach, affected by nausea, refuse it. Colorless? No. Definitely not colorless. Anything else. Red. Yes, bright red, clear so that it would not suggest blood.

She put some sweetening in it, some salt, a little alcohol.

Returning to the consulting room, she gave the large bottle to the woman and said: 'He'll taste salt. That's right. Salt helps to relieve cramp.'

Mrs Daley nodded. 'Yes. I've heard that. It's not nasty, is it? Beverley would never take anything nasty.'

'Apart from the salt, no. If he doesn't like it he can dilute it. Mrs Daley, I believe you when you say Beverley won't see me. But somebody will have to see him. I have a brother about Beverley's age. He's not a doctor. In fact, he's a fireman. If he called on you tomorrow, could you arrange for him to see Beverley?'

The woman considered the proposition suspiciously, but could find no reason to turn it down. After all, she really did want help for Beverley. Her love had not been enough. She had never been particularly keen on Beverley associating with boys his own age, but at least that was better than girls.

When she had gone, Anastasia phoned the fire station. But Conan had gone out on a call.

The tires had almost burned themselves out when a small red van arrived from Sherburn – a small van with only one man in it.

'You certainly took your time,' Sally said drily.

'I did, didn't I?' said Conan, who never argued without knowing what he was arguing about. 'What do you know about this? Anything? Or were you just passing?'

She pointed. 'That's my brother's car,' she said bleakly. 'Or it was.'

'You were with him?'

'I was in Sherburn, saw the smoke and cycled out.'

Conan Hersholt, after one glance told him there was not much to be done about the fire and not urgently, had been far more interested in Sally Wells than in the fire. He became even more interested now.

'You saw the smoke miles away and knew your brother was involved?'

'Not me, another girl. Arleen Jones.'

'Yet you're here and she isn't.'

'You're a fireman, aren't you? Are you going to do something about this?'

'There's not much to do, is there?'

'No,' she admitted. Her eyes were damp.

'Go and sit in the van.'

'I want to help.'

'You can't. Here – take a swig of this.' He took a flask from his pocket and handed it to her.

Sally had welcomed drink as she had welcomed sex, with open arms, and the outcome was similar – a resolution on her part to keep it in its place and be more discriminating in future. This, however, was a time for a stiff drink. She took it and was surprised to find it was not gin or whisky, but brandy.

'Go and sit in the van,' he repeated as she handed the flask back to him.

They looked at each other for a pregnant moment. Conan thought she was one of the prettiest girls he had ever seen, but more important than that – though he regarded it as quite important – she was no ordinary peasant. He could feel the forces of her personality although there was no elan.

That was strange. The moment of meeting was generally

the moment of recognition, and the elan was there even if the aura was lacking. Here there was aura and no elan. And of these four-letter words he had always regarded elan as more important, more definitive . . .

Apparently, too, the recognition was one-sided. She seemed to have sensed nothing in him. That, however, could be accounted for by the other emotions of the moment. Her brother had just been incinerated, and his funeral pyre was still burning.

Finally she nodded, and went and sat in the van. He had swung it round so that the rear doors were nearest the fire. Sitting in the front seat she faced the other way.

The van's equipment, such as it was, was not exactly designed for solo operation, but it had been designed in the knowledge that sometimes there would be only one man to handle it. Conan zipped himself into a fireproof suit and sprayed the smoking gorse, smothered the blazing rubber fragments which had burst from the car, and approached the black windowless shell. It was now possible to see inside the shell, the flames and smoke having died down, and he could see a gaunt and hideous object, still glowing red, which must have been the driver. Conan was glad the girl had not seen that.

There was nothing else to be done. Since the car could now burn itself out completely without fear of spreading, it was fire department policy to let it burn instead of extinguishing it and leaving still combustible debris to cause possible trouble later.

There was nothing else anyone would ever do, except that the girl would probably arrange for cremation of the body – ironic, that, since the job was virtually complete already. Burial was too costly and complicated. The cemeteries were disused and there were no gravediggers.

He went back to the van and told the girl: 'He died instantly. Broken neck.'

'Before the fire?'

'Before the fire.'

'I want to see.'

He shook his head definitely. 'You don't want to see.' He went to the side of the road, picked up her bicycle and put it in the back of the van. Then he got in beside her.

'That's all?' she said, surprised. 'You're not going to do any more?'

'The fire's practically out. The road's clear, the track is clear.'

'The car will be left there for ever?'

'Why not? It's a warning.'

She shuddered and moved closer to him.

It was a chance to be sure. Still no elan, but her aura, as expected, was much stronger now – a golden glow all about her, as if she were illuminated from within.

He knew perfectly well that while elan perception could be objective, aura was subjective, and she might look entirely different to another Norman. The golden glow was a cliché, accounted for perhaps entirely by her blonde head and red-gold skin. It was not, of course, a glow at all, since he could still see it if he shut his eyes.

His right hand touched her bare thigh gently while his left arm crept behind her. The way she moved under his interrogative touch, though she scarcely moved at all, told him one thing more: her sexual responses were far too quick and positive for her to be any ordinary girl.

And that needed to be proved, because the absence of elan meant she was a peasant while the golden aura insisted that she was not.

Like a Norman or possibly a Saxon (but she was no Saxon, obviously) and like no peasant, she was responding to him as a natural female . . . but when his touch became more insistent she flung him away with surprising strength. 'What the hell do you think you're doing?' she demanded, and then changed the mood and showed she had experience and a sense of humor by adding at once: 'Well, that was a silly thing to say. I know perfectly well what you're doing. Watch it, that's all.'

'You want it,' he said mildly.

'Get knotted,' she retorted rudely.

He smiled. They stayed apart, but she didn't jump out of the van or say anything that was manifestly untrue.

In a neutral tone he said: 'Yes, certainly we should know each other's names first. I'm Conan Hersholt.'

'Sally Wells. And if you think – '

'Tell me about this. What happened here?'

'I told you, I was miles away – '

'You know your brother. You can guess.'

'Oh . . . he probably raced the train, or something.'

'And miscalculated?'

'David never miscalculated. I mean he didn't make silly mistakes. An experiment might go wrong. If something caught his interest . . . he would take poison and then the antidote to see if it worked. That's what he was like.'

'So he wasn't like you.'

'What do you know about me?'

He merely smiled.

'No,' she said at last. 'He wasn't like me. I had to look after him.'

Conan knew somehow that the dead man had been about twenty-five, his own age. Sally couldn't be less than seventeen or more than nineteen. Yet she had had to look after David.

Anastasia had had to look after him, too. But she was older, she had money, education, experience, high intelligence. It was no shame for Conan to be looked after for most of his life by Anastasia (he believed that now he was looking after her). There was some shame in David having to be looked after by his little sister.

'This Arleen Jones. You say she *knew*?'

Sally would have liked to talk with somebody else about the strange fur in strange places on Arleen's body, and it would not have bothered her to discuss it with a man. However, she had just repulsed a too-quick, too-blatant advance by Conan, and she had no intention of entering into any frank sexual discussion with him that might start him off again.

'Yes, she knew. She knew where to look for the smoke and she knew what the smoke meant. I don't care for that sort of thing, but after all it was David. I had to come and look.'

'That sort of thing?'

'Spiritualism, fortune-telling, reading cards, palmistry, astrology – '

'You class them all together?'

'Don't you?'

'No. I've never got a message from beyond the grave. I'm not much interested in whether you're Gemini or Aquarius. But

Arleen Jones, from what you've said yourself, has something that really works.'

'Obviously.' She shrugged her shoulders, still not greatly interested.

He started the motor and they didn't speak again until they reached the town.

Now that he had met Sally he had no intention of losing her. Soon they would make love, and perhaps after that there would be elan. Soon . . . Conan didn't know whether that meant hours or days or weeks, but it was inevitable, since he wanted it and Sally was not a peasant.

She didn't know much of the truth, if any of it, which meant she had somehow managed to stay clear of both Normans and Saxons. Unlikely as that seemed, it could be explained by the fact that there was no elan.

And having known only peasants (her brother was obviously a peasant) she had not begun to live. Conan had genuinely expected her, after that automatic move toward him, to let him make love to her. Now that virility was so rare, the men who were truly men and the women who were truly women were drawn together more compulsively than ever before in history. There was an inevitability about it there had never been. The concept of faithfulness was dissolving . . . the possibility of real sexual experience went beyond exclusiveness.

'Where do you live?' he asked as they turned off the motorway at the fringes of Sherburn. The outskirts were dreary and dilapidated – with a falling population, it was always the outskirts of a town which were first abandoned to decay.

'Here,' she said.

'Here?' he echoed incredulously. It was impossible. Her clothes, exiguous as they were, were immaculate, even elegant. She could not live in squalor and decay.

'Chestnut Drive,' she said. 'First right.' And thirty seconds later he stopped the van outside her house.

It was possible after all. In a street of derelict, tumbledown villas which had once been identical, one was as immaculate as Sally's powder-blue shorts suit. The garden was simple but well-kept. There was a gravel drive to an open, empty garage. Sally wheeled her bicycle towards it but didn't put it inside.

She leaned the machine against the side of the garage and slammed the door with finality.

'You live alone,' said Conan, who was a step behind her.

'Yes, except for David . . . ' She stopped, and the tears started. Just started. She didn't have to check them. They checked themselves.

'You'll be alone now, tonight, Sally?'

'Yes,' she said with firm finality, answering a different question from the one he had asked. 'And the name is Miss Wells.'

The phone in the house was ringing. That was a small pointer, the fact that out here, on the outskirts of town, she had a phone and it was working. You generally had to maintain your own phone link these days.

'Arleen Jones,' he said casually. 'Hair?'

The way she jerked answered him. The way she stared confirmed that she didn't know what it meant.

'That's your phone,' he said. 'So long, Miss Wells.'

As he turned to go he had a sudden clear premonition, as if he had been a Saxon. *He and Sally would never make love.* It was a disturbing thought, for he still had every intention that it would happen and he knew that Sally had no very great objection to the idea. If the premonition was true, and it had the feeling of truth, did that mean that either he or Sally was to die soon, before their relationship could progress farther?

Sally never let a phone go on ringing. She made no unnecessary calls herself and always thought any call might be vital. She accepted the farewell although if the phone had not been ringing she would certainly have asked questions.

It was Arleen on the line. Sally said: 'Yes, it's David. The car's burned out. No, there isn't any doubt.'

Arleen waited for no more. There was a click.

Sally turned back to the open door. If Conan had still been there she would have asked him about the significance of his sudden laconic question. Was there a correlation between excessive body hair and precognition, or whatever it was? Were there others like Arleen? Was he himself covered by a light down, and was that how he knew about Arleen?

But Conan and the red van were gone.

With a conscious effort she recalled all that she knew of

his appearance. Concerned only about David, she had paid no particular attention to Conan. However, his visual recall was excellent.

Conan was not tall, not much taller than she was. His face, now that she thought about it, presented some remarkable contrasts. It was rugged in contour yet his skin was as smooth as hers. He was quiet, ordinary, yet there was strength in his face. His tunic had been open at the neck, and his throat and chest, though brown, were conspicuously hairless.

No, he wasn't hairy. On the contrary, she now found it strange that his chin was so smooth, as if he had just that moment had a very close shave. The hair on his head, too, was thin – not sparse as if he was prematurely going bald, but very fine and silky, like a girl's.

So much of him was like a girl, yet there was no doubt of his masculinity.

Sally knew it was necessary to see him again, and soon. She almost wished she had let him make love to her . . . although she did not love him she would not mind making love to him.

But she had never entered on a casual sex relationship. The euphemism 'intimacy' meant something after all. It seemed to her unreasonable, even disgusting, to share the ultimate physical experience with a stranger, when all that was needed to transform him from a stranger was a little patience.

The coincidence was not remarkable. Conan, after all, was a fireman, and fire was the link between him and David and Arleen.

He returned to the station and went out on two routine calls.

The third was to the shop of Sally Wells in Cornwall Place. The name was not uncommon, but could Sally be a shopkeeper?

When the van drew up outside the shop, he found the usual staring crowd clustered around it. The fire was not in the shop nor in the flat above it. It was in the flat above that, and there were no flames, only smoke gushing from the windows.

The shop was closed, locked, but there was, also as usual, a bystander who knew everything. A tall, seedy man with a drooping mustache, he obviously had no intention of taking any action himself.

'That's the door at the side there,' he said. 'It leads to both flats. We had a look in, but the stairs are full of smoke. Nobody lives in the flat above the shop. Top floor, the shop girl lives there.'

'The girl who owns the shop?' Conan had a moment of fear. Sally had had time to come here and . . .

'No, that's Sally Wells, she ain't here. The girl that works in the shop has the top flat. Tall, dark girl. Arleen Jones.'

Arleen Jones . . . Conan devoutly hoped that she was a Saxon or a peasant, not a Norman. Suppose – he thought of it only now – that when he surprised Sally with the key word 'hair' and she reacted, the fact had been that Arleen was singularly lacking in hair? Unusually, unnaturally lacking?

He wasted no time. He put on his helmet and his mask, his coat, and took his axe and a cylinder of foam.

The stairs were indeed full of smoke, but there was no flame. He dashed up one flight, two flights. The door at the top was locked. Two blows with the axe shattered the lock.

Inside, the smoke was denser than ever. He was almost blind in spite of his mask. And still there was no flame. Then, in the bedroom, flame too, but not much. A clumsy attempt had been made to set a mattress on fire, bedclothes, a divan, a dressing-table. He recognized the signs. Not an accidental fire, a deliberate one.

Many of the materials piled together, however, were non-combustible or slow-burning. He sprayed the seat of the blaze until he was satisfied the fire would go out, though there was going to be a lot more smoke.

He found the girl in the kitchen, on the floor. She had evidently been in the bedroom and had intended to remain there to die, but had been forced by an irrepressible instinct of self-preservation to get away from the choking smoke, to make for an open window.

She was unmarked, and as Conan slammed the bedroom door on the dying fire within and the smoke in the rest of the apartment slowly cleared, he saw that not as much as a fingertip or any part of her dark clothes was singed.

But she was quite dead – asphyxiated. Conan, a Norman, did not have to search for her pulse or listen for her heartbeat. Nor did he waste time on the kiss of life.

Conan knew far better than his doctor sister when a person was dead.

At the same time the total absence of elan, aura, even more rudimentary traces of personality, made it impossible to tell what she had been. It was therefore necessary, while he was quite alone with the body, cut off from any possibility of interference from outside by the smoke which still filled the stairs, to make absolutely sure what she was. As he lifted her gently on to a couch he eased the dark sweater off her body and pulled off her pants.

She was a typical, undoubted, undeniable Saxon.

Her breasts were large, smooth and pale, and below them there was dark fur everywhere except over the navel. She was not naked any more than a cat or a dog or a horse could be naked. Nor was her lightly-furred body unattractive. Indeed, the one thing which spoiled the natural animal beauty of her body was the fact that she had shaved her arms and shoulders bare, obviously in order not to be detected as a Saxon in ordinary everyday intercourse with peasants or Normans.

The police, the ambulancemen and the undertakers would find out about this, of course. Not for the first time he pondered over the fragility of the secrecy that both Normans and Saxons uneasily maintained over their slight physical differences from the peasants. Who knew? Who did not know? Were both Normans and Saxons wasting their time hiding among the peasants, pretending to *be* peasants?

Nevertheless, they had to go on. There were so few of them. A secret could always be revealed, but once revealed, could not be made a secret again.

Carefully he restored her clothes so that no fur showed. The police and others could assume if they liked that the fireman who was first on the scene had noticed nothing. The doctor, when he saw Arleen, could assume if he liked that neither the fireman nor the police knew of anything out of the ordinary about the girl.

And so it could go on until some child pointed and shrilled: 'Look! The emperor isn't wearing any clothes!'

Not two hundred yards away from Sally's house, but in a different street, a battered car pulled up outside a much seedier house than hers. In this street, incredibly named Chestnut Grove, all the houses were empty except the one outside which the car stopped, and it looked more forlorn than the rest.

Nobody would have been likely to guess from the appearance of the passenger in the car, a short, flabby man in cheap, ill-fitting clothes, that the street was empty because he had bought all the houses in it, and that he had bought the street simply for privacy.

The driver, a tall young man with very light blue eyes and an expressionless face, held the door open for his passenger, standing erect like a guardsman.

'I've told you not to do that!' the short man said irritably. 'You look like a chauffeur. Anybody seeing us – '

'Sorry, Mr Gardner. I wasn't thinking.'

'Then think, damn you!'

The tall man's manner, however, did not change. The many strange relationships between Arthur Gardner and Vince Hobley made sometimes one, sometimes the other, the leading partner. And they made the bond between them quite indissoluble.

Sometimes Vince, who was after all the servant, the dependant, chose to be abjectly servile. Sometimes he chose to be arrogant, forcing Gardner to acknowledge that for all his power and wealth Vince was as much the master as he was.

At the dilapidated door, slightly off its hinges, it was Vince who produced a key and threw the door open. He stood aside, almost bowing, to allow Gardner to enter, and then followed him. Without appearing to hurry, he passed the other man in the hall and was in position to throw an inner door open and switch on the lights. There was pleasure, small pleasure, in irritating Gardner in this way.

Stone steps led downwards to another door.

The house was small and had never, even in its better days, provided more than minimum-standard living accommodation. It had never had a cellar. The cellar had been dug out afterwards.

The door at the bottom of the steps was a very curious door. It was made of iron, a solid, rusty slab of metal with no attempt at ornamentation. Vince produced two keys and shot two bolts at top and bottom of the door, standing aside to let Gardner enter first.

The cellar was a torture chamber, furnished with apparatus ancient and modern, but mostly ancient, for the infliction of pain. Gardner's taste in sadism and masochism was not subtle. Whether inflicting or enjoying torment, he liked it at its most bloody and brutal.

There was a rack, a genuine Spanish Inquisition model. There was a tall Iron Maiden, open, showing the spikes inside. There was block and tackle apparatus for strappado, a bed of coals for heating pincers and branding irons, a footcrusher, thumbscrews, several whipping-posts, a rack of long knives, a curiously curved blade which had been used for evisceration, a ducking-stool (but no water), a case of canes. Chains were attached to the stone walls. There was a modern water heater to supply live steam, and adjustable surgical table on which strange operations could be performed, a powerful pump to provide water jets at high pressure.

It was a temple dedicated to man's inhumanity to man. Some of the ancient devices had not been used for a long time, and never in this cellar. The Iron Maiden was too final for Gardner's tastes. He liked to look at it, but he had never stood inside it, and on the few occasions when he and Vince had found a human derelict so worthless to anybody that he could be done to death with little fear of the consequences, Gardner could always think of something better to do with him than simply putting him in the Iron Maiden and slamming the door.

Gardner liked to *see* what was happening.

Other devices, however, were in current use. Some of the blood on the filthy stone floor was not old.

Gardner made a slow, contented survey of the torture chamber. It had cost him five times as much as the street outside to build and furnish. And it was worth every penny.

He turned to Hobley. 'The doctor?'

'All arranged, Mr Gardner.'

'The time? How long before she'll be here?'

'You told me not to tell you,' said Vince with mild reproof. 'You don't want to know.'

'This time I have to know. I want the whip. Nothing but the whip. But I don't want to die.'

'Naturally.'

'I can't take more than twenty minutes.'

And I'll make it seem like a century, Vince thought. But of course this was really up to him, not Gardner. It was Vince's duty and privilege to inflict all the pain his perverted employer craved, all he could take, more than he could take . . . but do nothing that the doctor, when she arrived, could not restore.

'You leave it to me, Mr Gardner,' he said soothingly.

Anastasia was putting on her coat when Conan came in.

'A call?' he said, surprised, for like most doctors she seldom went out on calls, doing most of her work in her surgery or at the hospital.

'Yes. The Beast.'

'Oh.' He knew all about the Beast, though for reasons of old-fashioned professional secrecy Anastasia had never told him his name. 'I suppose you have to do work like that?'

She shrugged. 'Not everybody pays. I need a few who not only pay, but pay a lot. Anyway, it's not unethical. By the time I arrive he or his victim always needs treatment, which I have to give.'

'A nice point. At the time the appointment is made, medical attention isn't necessary. Though you know it will be by the time you get there.'

She shrugged again, her conscience evidently easy. 'If it were within my power to stop it, my attitude might be different. But consent covers most things short of homicide and suicide. If I'd reported the Beast last week when he was indulging the sadistic half of his nasty nature by doing certain unpleasant things to a poor girl who needed the money – if I'd sent the police instead of going myself, the girl would have insisted that it was all her idea. Anyway, Con, there's something else I want to talk about. You're off duty now?'

'Have been since before the last two fires.'

'Tomorrow morning too?'

'Morning, yes. I'm not due at the station until noon.'

'I want you to see somebody for me. Beverley Daley. He's

about your age, won't see doctors, particularly women doctors. He might see you.'

'I'm no doctor.'

'It's as much a case for a fireman as for a doctor.'

He smiled. 'What kind of case is that? And by the way, don't you have to hurry? Isn't there a chance that by the time you turn up, you might be too late?'

'No,' she said indifferently. 'The Beast is having himself worked over tonight. There's nothing else about him healthy, but his heart is as sound as a bell. Sometimes, when I know he's the victim, I deliberately turn up late. He enjoys being hurt, of course, or he wouldn't do it. But the enjoyment depends on the knowledge that soon I'm going to turn up and restore him. I like to give him a few minutes of fright. Maybe he's got a crushed foot. Maybe he's bleeding from a thousand cuts. Maybe I won't turn up at all. Now, Beverley Daley – '

'Yes. Not a case for a doctor, you said.'

'Much more a case for you. He's dying of thirst. Go and pump water into him.'

'Huh?'

'His mother described all the early symptoms of death by thirst. Loss of appetite, terror, nausea, cramps, giddiness, headaches. Dry mouth, swollen tongue. Itching. Delirium. Next, if something isn't done about it, there'll be deafness and blindness. Then his skin will go blue. Soon he won't bleed when you cut him – the blood will be so thick it'll dry up.'

'I don't understand. Why can't he drink?'

'Of course he can drink. He does drink, or his mother would have spotted the real reason for his illness long before now. He just doesn't drink enough, that's all.'

'Some secondary illness? Diabetes, or – '

'I don't think so. He just refuses to drink enough. It's the first time I've encountered this. But I've a feeling it won't be the last.'

He nodded slowly. 'I begin to get the idea. Just another form of suicide. People who stop eating aren't uncommon. This one presumably eats, but not drinking enough would make him eat less – '

'Exactly. The death wish is probably unconscious. He's not consciously abstaining from water to kill himself. He's not consciously committing suicide. He's just cutting down on something which he needs to go on living.'

'What have you done about it?'

'Given him a pleasant mixture that will make him thirsty. Perhaps he'll take it. Perhaps it'll make him drink. If not, it's up to you. I told you it's not a medical problem.'

He nodded. 'I'll go.'

'And I'd better go too, just in case my patient really is bleeding to death.'

Gardner was not bleeding to death; he was supremely happy.

Vince Hobley was proud of his skill with the whip. Not for him heavy brutal flesh-mangling lashes which would send Gardner into unresponsive oblivion within seconds.

Gardner, stripped to the waist, his arms tied around the whipping post, was scarcely marked. His pudgy back was raw only in one tender spot between the shoulder-blades. And Vince was flicking the raw spot delicately, at precise intervals. There was something of the Chinese water torture in the treatment. Gardner's agony was exquisite . . . but he had not uttered a sound.

Vince was also bare to the waist. Flesh-colored fur matted his chest and covered his back nearly to the shoulders. His arms, too, were heavily furred. Only his neck, upper shoulders and rib cavity were pale and hairless.

Gardner's black body hair was patchy, like that on his head. Where it grew, it was longer and thicker than Vince's. Where it didn't grow, he was pinky naked.

Vince, no longer enjoying himself so much, was silently pleading for just one scream from his master. Vince had to win. He could not take defeat, and Gardner was defeating him by staying silent, though Vince had already told him that the doctor was five minutes late. 'She may be a long time yet, Mr Gardner. Maybe she isn't coming at all. Maybe she's forgotten.'

Vince had not failed to notice that Dr Anastasia Hersholt was liable to turn up slightly early when she knew Gardner was working on somebody else, and at other times slightly late.

Suddenly furious, determined to achieve the victory of a scream from Gardner, Vince lashed out with all his strength, savagely, abandoning subtlety, once, twice, three times.

Gardner, his back now running with blood, did not utter a sound. He lapsed into unconsciousness, hanging from the ropes but not a murmur was drawn from him.

And Vince had lost.

He wanted to scream in frustration, but that would make the defeat still worse. It would be an admission of his defeat, and Vince, who could not bear to lose, was even less able to acknowledge that he had lost.

The buzzer behind the iron door sounded. That meant the doctor was on her way down. Vince moved to the door, then turned to pick up his shirt and put it on, buttoning it to the throat.

Hobley did not like to be seen naked or half naked. When the fur started to grow a few years ago – long after puberty – he had at first been secretly proud of it, regarding it as proof of virility . . . though as he told himself confidently, and with some excuse, there was no need for proof. But when he began to find people staring at him, whispering, turning away, he became selfconscious. He no longer took pleasure in baring his strong, spare body. Only with Gardner and a few others, some of them furred like himself, did he reveal himself. They didn't whisper and turn away. They liked it.

He began to take women by force, by intent. Previously he had had no need of force. They were nearly all willing. When some, not all, became unwilling, shrank from him, his ego demanded that he should never risk refusal. He would never talk, never ask, never beg, never reveal himself. He would take his women by force, in the dark. His fur was so soft, so fine, that they never knew for sure he was not an ordinary man. Any man could have hair on his chest, his legs, particularly on his private parts.

Sometimes he forgot his resolution and found himself weakly begging. But he always won in the end.

Or so he told himself.

Of course the doctor knew about Gardner's hair, but as it happened Gardner could just pass as a particularly hairy peasant. Anyway, what the doctor thought about Gardner didn't matter to Vince, who cared only about what people thought of himself.

When he let her in, Anastasia didn't speak. There was nothing to say. And in the torture chamber she didn't even look around. It was an old story.

She checked the pulse of the still unconscious man, gave him a shot to keep him out for another hour, and then Vince laid him face down on the surgical table.

It was not necessary to clean the wounds. The electrorestorer which Anastasia used was man's greatest and perhaps final technological achievement. Cells had always been capable of replacing themselves. Cells even had the near-miraculous property of being able to take over the functions of different adjoining cells. Human cells were defeated only by burning, which was in effect destruction.

It was significant that Gardner never had himself burned in his pursuit of the pleasures of pain.

The electrorestorer made cells work fast. Though a vast breakthrough, it was nothing really new – the body itself still did all the healing. True, the electrorestorer drained and exhausted the body and in some cases, instead of curing, it could kill. But these were not cases of well-nourished, overfed bodies, which benefited greatly from the treatment, giving their owners a chance to start from scratch and overfeed them again. It was as good as the exercise they would not take.

Anastasia set the many clamps expertly, watched silently by Vince. It was a highly skilled job and not many doctors were masters of it. In time, perhaps, man's greatest achievement would be lost simply because there was nobody left with the skill to operate it – even before the machines themselves broke down.

When all the clamps were in place and fastened to the slave unit, Anastasia sprayed the entire healing area with a pink mist which set rapidly to the consistency of soft jelly.

Then she turned away. 'Three hours should do it,' she said. 'The clamps will drop off – you know. Don't clean off the jelly. Leave it on overnight. Drop the machine at my surgery as usual.'

Vince nodded.

'Of course the healing won't be complete for a couple of weeks, even with this treatment. There may be faint scars –'

She stopped, not only because he knew this as well as she did but because he was obviously thinking of something completely different. When he touched her arm gently, she knew what it was.

Surprised, she looked at him keenly. His virility was not in doubt, and this made him an object of interest to her, since the only other man she knew whose virility was never in doubt was her brother. In Sherburn less than half the male population achieved full potency even at the height of their youth, health and strength. Male impotence, or more generally periodicity, had long been treated by women as permission to seek solace elsewhere. It was no longer hard for any virile man to get girls. The snag was that more than half of them, too, had little to offer in the way of sexual response.

For his part, Vince saw a woman who took great care of herself, who, in her middle thirties at least, had the shape of a young girl and an elegance that no young girl had had time to learn. There was artistry in the way her long blonde hair was arranged, and it was her artistry, not that of a stylist. Her neat blue suit had been made for her and no one else . . . there was a touch of genius about the way it fitted that showed it could never have come off the peg.

And as he was reacting, allowing himself to react to her subtle, mature allure, seeing himself her lover within the next couple of minutes, she said coolly: 'I appreciate the offer, but no. I do my own choosing.'

Surprised and angry, he wished (as he did far more often than he would ever admit to himself) that he had not made the move, that he had not risked refusal. Mistakenly, he had not thought it much of a risk. A woman who did what this woman did for Gardner could not be a paragon.

And then he thought, what did it matter? True, she knew him, he could not take her unknown, in the dark, as he liked to take women. But that was of little account. The weak, harassed forces of law and order never bothered with simple rape, uncommon anyway, only violation with violence. Overpower her, tear the elegant clothes from her elegant body, take her, being careful only to leave no mark on her, and nobody would ever do anything about it.

She had a tiny silver pistol in her hand. 'I told you,' she

said firmly. 'I appreciate the offer. I've been very polite. Don't force me to be rude.'

He cursed and stepped back. And made the inevitable resolution that somehow, some day, she would pay.

The young girl reporter of the *Sherburn Weekly*, which sometimes did manage to come out weekly but more often than not was delayed by some production problem or other, was sent out to cover the fire at the Cornwall Place shop.

She was determined to get a big story. If it didn't turn out to be a big story, she would probe and pry and persist and then write up the fruits of her labor so brilliantly and with such searing honesty that she would make it a big story. She *cared.*

At first they wouldn't even let her see the dead girl, but eventually she got all the facts, and knew she really had a big story.

She wrote it wildly and incoherently, letting her imagination take charge.

When he read it, the editor of the *Sherburn Weekly* picked up the phone.

'I've got to talk with Meredith Dundee personally,' he insisted. 'Of course it's important. You know that. How often do I call him?'

After a long pause Meredith Dundee came to the phone. He was not pleased. 'I was in the pool,' he grumbled. 'What is it now?'

A moment later, however, his grumble was forgotten. 'You did right to call me,' he said. 'The story? No, don't kill it. Just the bit about the new race, the hair. Get a paper out tomorrow . . . Run the fire story exactly like any other fire in which a young woman died, give it no more and no less. The funeral? Keep quiet about that. I'll arrange it. There may be rumors, we can't kill rumors, but there won't be any definite information.'

'Fire the girl?' the editor suggested.

'Don't be a bloody fool. That would prove she was being muzzled. Just tell her that the *Sherburn Weekly* isn't a spicy rag exploiting the misfortunes of freaks, especially unfortunate dead freaks. Send her on another job, an interesting job, and splash whatever she turns in.'

'Yes, Mr Dundee. Is that all?'

'Yes . . . no. Call that uncle of yours, the undertaker, and get him to pick up the girl Jones. Right away. Bills to me – no, to you, and I'll settle with you in cash.'

The editor did as he was told, and his uncle did as he was told.

The uncle, the undertaker, forced to call out two men and a van, remembered the earlier call. He had told a Miss Sally Wells that there was no chance of sending anyone to pick up the body of her brother that day. But if the van was going out anyway, it might as well pick up the two bodies.

Curious, that. Both deaths caused by fire, though miles apart. David Wells, and Arleen Jones at one of the Wells shops. They must have known each other.

That night David and Arleen lay together, for the first and last time . . . in a restroom.

2

Sally awoke from uneasy sleep feeling cold, with a bad taste in her mouth, an uneasy stomach and a trace of a sick headache. All these things were practically unknown to her. She blamed the brandy she had drunk the day before. And then, because she hated being deceived by herself or anybody else, she admitted that she had not been able to dismiss David from her mind.

She told herself firmly that David was dead and that she had to get used to the idea. It had to happen. For a while it would be best not even to think about David.

She jumped out of bed, wincing. She winced again in the shower, but deliberately turned it to cold. After forcing herself to drink a glass of milk, she put on a clean sweater and shorts and sandals, shut the house and went for a run on her bicycle.

Nobody had called to tell her that an employee of hers had died in a fire over one of her shops. The mills of administration now ground exceeding slow and not very small.

Arthur Gardner saw her, and watched her cycle the length of Chestnut Grove.

He too had spent an uncomfortable night. One of the clamps refused to detach, as sometimes happened when the healing did not go as rapidly and smoothly as expected. (Perhaps, too, the skilful Dr Anastasia Hersholt had not been as skilful as usual.) Vince and Gardner slept at the house, and Gardner got up, at last feeling good, when the clamp finally detached itself, just in time to watch Sally Wells cycle down the empty street.

He had seen her before, for Chestnut Grove, the street he owned, was on her way out of what had once been a housing estate. He knew where she lived but didn't know her name. There was a brother, and Gardner had had trouble with brothers before. He preferred orphans without brothers, sisters or lovers.

However, feeling on top of the world, he was excited by the sight of the girl . . . young, pretty, active, lightly clad. First, perhaps, he would possess her, though such episodes were becoming rarer. He didn't know it, but perversion was now becoming normality for him and straightforward things like sex without perversion no longer had a place in his life. Then, the delights of working on that small, well-formed body.

Vince was at his elbow. 'Did you see her?' Gardner demanded.

'Yes.'

'Get her for me, Hobley.'

'There's a brother – '

'I know there's a brother! They'll want money. Everybody wants money. Square the brother first. Then get the girl.'

'With her written consent, of course.'

'Get her any way you like.'

'When?'

'Now, right now! Take the car. I'll walk home. You'll easily catch up with her. She's taking the road out of town.'

Turning onto the motorway, Sally did not notice the blue sign forbidding cyclists, pedestrians, learner drivers, motor cycles of less than 50 c.c., invalid carriages, agricultural vehicles and animals using the motorway. She had never seen it: it was like many other signs, still in position and legible, which had long since ceased to mean anything.

She had no wish to see the burned-out car again, and it was not necessary. Only a mile along the motorway a narrow road led away from the freeway to a group of villages, Davenport, Elton and Highwood. She knew them well.

Physical wellbeing had returned. And the sun came out. Soon she was so warm from the exertion, though wearing only a thin yellow sweater and blue sailcloth shorts, that she slowed to an easier pace.

On what was virtually a country lane, Sally encountered

nothing and no one, except one following car. Nobody got up early any more, not even in the countryside. The cattle and poultry and fields had to wait.

Her bicycle was well maintained and silent. She had heard the car even before she turned off the highway and was not surprised when it followed her. There were villages and farms on the minor roads, nothing on the big highway. She was, however surprised that it didn't pass her.

Thinking that perhaps the car was staying behind because the road was so narrow it would be difficult to pass even a bicycle, she turned off at the track to the river. Aglow now with her customary wellbeing, she was conscious of two minor discomforts. She was still hot and she was hungry. A quick swim in the river would cure the first and intensify the second, which was fine as there was a farm only a mile further on with which she had dealings. Most of the farms which supplied her with dairy products were farther away. It was easy for farms so near Sherburn to sell their products, and to get a better deal she generally had to go farther afield. All the same, it was well known that Sally Wells was always prepared to take any farm produce at a reasonable price, unlike most of the other dealers, who wanted only what was virtually sold already. There were few farms with which Sally had not done business, and at Crofton she could get a solid homely meal and perhaps do a deal on the side.

When she heard the car still following her down the track to the river, there was no longer any doubt.

Sally did not dress provocatively to be provocative. She liked having her arms and legs bare and they generally were. It was not the first time she had been followed by a car with a man or men in it. If she had to fight, it would not be the first time either.

She could handle most men who were on their own simply because she was prepared to take more than they were. When a pimply youth slapped her on the face, he thought that would end her resistance. Her small hard fist applied forcefully changed his mind on that, but not his conviction that establishing his superiority and his right of conquest was only a matter of time. As time passed, however, and he was hurt more and more, and Sally became more, not less determined, his conviction weakened. Even when he hurt Sally more than she hurt him, he didn't see it that way . . . So in such encounters Sally had only once been the loser.

That time she had been quite resigned, quite philosophical. She meant to go on fighting to the end, but she was going to lose. A realist, she saw that.

But the wouldbe Romeo had exhausted himself. And for a moment, before she laughed and jeered and drove him from her in hot shame, she was annoyed. It was not that she wanted to be raped. It was rather that she had made up her mind to it, a new experience, and was ready for it.

Two or more men she ran from, if necessary. But there was only one man in this car.

On the rutted track, dry and stony, she made better time than the car. The driver had to have some care for his suspension. She put as much distance as possible between herself and the car, not to get away, for the track led nowhere else, but to give her time to hide her bicycle. If she had to take to the bushes or the river, the man in the car was quite likely to smash her cycle from spite, and then she'd have a long walk home.

She reached the riverside and turned left. A narrow path ran for only a hundred yards or so before ending in impenetrable undergrowth. People from the farms occasionally fished from the river bank at this point.

Jumping off her machine, she lifted it easily and forced her way a few hundred yards into the thick bushes and trees. The ground was bone dry and her tires had left no tracks. She hid the bicycle under a bush and let the branches swing back over it. Although a really determined search would no doubt uncover her machine, she didn't expect any such industry. The kind of youths she generally had to deal with would throw her bicycle into the river if it was in plain view, but would not spend time and energy beating the bushes searching for it.

Then she returned to the path and went on to the end of it, where she sat by the water's edge.

The car reached the end of the track and stopped. A man came out.

As he came toward her, Sally watched him calmly and curiously. Instinct told her she could never get on with this man. He was no youth. He must be around twenty-eight. He had very pale blue eyes, eyes she distrusted. Though roughly dressed in a coarse dark shirt and shapeless jeans he was clean, not bad-looking. But she didn't like him. She would never like him.

She considered jumping into the river and swimming away, just to annoy him, and would have done it but for the fact that she didn't want to get her clothes and particularly her shoes wet.

Vince watched her and guessed what she intended.

'If you're thinking of jumping in,' he said when he was about ten yards from her, 'don't try it. I'm a pretty good swimmer myself.'

'Stay where you are,' she said, and was slightly surprised when he obeyed. 'Why should I jump in, anyway?'

'Exactly, why should you? I'm Vince Hobley. I think your name is Sally?'

'So?'

Her breasts did not have the brash, belligerent contours that would have been given by an uplift bra. The lines, though firm, were more natural, and the shape of small nipples showed. It was almost impossible not to make a pass at her on his own behalf. But Gardner wouldn't like that. He was here, after all, as Gardner's emissary, and there was no way of wrapping up what he had to say as Gardner's representative.

'Would you like to earn some money?' Vince said. 'Quite a lot of money?'

'Doing what?'

'Being the playmate of an old, fat, rich pervert.'

'What does playmate mean?'

'Exactly what you think. Plus letting him do certain other things to you.'

'Crawl back under your stone,' said Sally.

'Am I to take it you absolutely refuse?'

'Yes.'

'And there's no possibility of making you change your mind?'

'None.'

Then there was no reason why he shouldn't make a pass at her himself. The cool refusal of the cool Anastasia still rankled. This girl could make him feel good again.

A warning bell rang in his mind. This girl looked as determined as Dr Anastasia Hersholt – more determined. He did not want to risk another defeat.

But Sally had no pistol. He could see that. He could take her as he liked – violently, roughly, against her will. He advanced again.

Cautiously, watching him closely, Sally got to her feet. It was possible, though not likely, that he could swim as well as he said. By going into the water she might be placing herself at a disadvantage.

At the last moment he changed his tactics and rushed her. She grabbed his wrist, got under him, and skill discounted his fifty per cent advantage in weight. He sailed over her head into the river, landing on his back.

He *was* a good swimmer. She saw that by the way he was out of the river and coming at her again within seconds. She went for his right wrist again, didn't get it this time, caught his shirt instead, swung him off balance and with a vigorous thrust of her knee tumbled him back in the river.

When he climbed out again, furious, she saw the fur. His shirt was torn and for the second time in twenty-four hours she saw hair where no hair should be – the hair this time that proclaimed a male Saxon.

Sally didn't like hairy men.

He expected her to try to prevent him climbing out, or let him out and then devote all her efforts to doing what she had already done twice, throwing him back in the river. This gave her the chance to do what she intended the last time. She seized his right wrist, turned swiftly and exerted all the pressure she could on it, using her shoulder as a fulcrum. Then she pulled it sharply, twisted it, tripped him and rolled with him, never releasing his wrist. A further lever and she had accomplished what she set out to do – both a muscle strain and a small bone break.

When she released him he stood back, angry, grimacing and massaging his wrist.

He did not rush her again. He was heavier and much stronger than she was, and now, more wary, he was sure he would be able to overcome her, fully fit. But he was no longer fully fit, and she was skilled in judo, his own experience of which was rudimentary and entirely theoretical. With a useless wrist it would be foolish to go against her.

'One day,' he said with controlled passion, 'I'll kill you for that.'

Sally laughed, though it wasn't very funny. She knew he meant it. But she had to stay on the offensive. If she gave the slightest sign of weakening, even now, he would probably go for her again and might win this time.

'I won't be able to drive,' he said.

'You should have thought of that before. Anyway, I'm sure you will, though you won't find it pleasant. And the sooner you get started the better.'

Vince was a stronger man than most. Yet there was a deep well of fear in him. He feared tackling Sally again because he feared he would lose. The fact that he had started with all the advantages made it worse. To be beaten by a man twice his size was nothing. To be beaten by a girl half his size was everything.

A strange fancy seized him. He wished he had rushed Anastasia and she had shot and killed him. That would not have been defeat. That would have been victory.

To rush this girl now would bring defeat and it could not bring victory.

Without another word he turned and trudged back to the car, still nursing his wrist. He had considerable difficulty in getting the car turned. When he had succeeded, Sally listened intently and was convinced the car did not stop before getting back to the road.

He might return. It would be easy for him to creep back silently to the riverside, a jack or a wheelbrace in his left hand, and attack her only when he was certain of success. She did not, however, think this was likely. She had caught a hint of fear in his light blue eyes and guessed at what was behind it, the man's terror of losing his self-esteem. As things were, he could convince himself she had won the encounter because he had taken her too lightly, which was true. He didn't want to take the chance of losing this excuse.

Left alone, she threw off her clothes and dived into the river. It was the river Terne, which emerged from Sherburn broad, fast and not very clean. Here, however, above the town, it was narrow, slow and crystal-clear. She could see the trout darting in its depths. Few anglers came here, and they were mostly from the surrounding farms. Better supplied with prime meat and vegetables than town dwellers, they fished for sport rather than food, and the fish, once nearly exterminated by pollution and overfishing, multiplied.

Sally, a distance swimmer rather than a sprinter, swam lazily upstream, knowing that if she got tired she could simply float back to where she started. She had swum here before once or twice, not often, and after the brief exhilaration of disposing of Vince she swam farther than before and found an island she had not previously seen.

It was little more than a sandbank on which a few scraggy bushes had taken precarious hold. It was of no great interest except that a naked girl was diving from it, swimming back to the island and diving again.

Something made Sally halt, tread water and watch her. The girl, unlike Vince, represented no threat to her nor she to the girl. Yet something told Sally – who was not superstitious and did not have strange feelings or hunches or premonitions – to watch rather than swim right up to the girl and say hello.

It might have been what the girl was doing . . . but that was swiftly explained. She was no more than a fair swimmer, and her dives, always from the same spot where she knew there was deep water, were erratic. Some were almost perfect and others poor. She was teaching herself to swim and dive. As Sally was well aware, it wasn't easy to find someone to teach you judo or swimming or climbing – you had to find out from books and by trial and error.

It was hardly surprising that the girl did not notice Sally, treading water and watching her . . . but as Sally edged nearer, it did become a little surprising. Sally guessed the girl was short-sighted. There was something about the way that short-sighted people not wearing glasses peered about them that could be spotted from quite a long way off by people blessed with perfect sight.

The girl's age was puzzling. She was obviously young, younger than Sally, and at first Sally, for no good reason, put her age at nine or ten. But she was too big to be nine or ten. And her breasts, though small, were fully developed.

Perhaps it was the fact that she was totally hairless except for the short dark hair on her head that had made Sally take her at first for a child. Few women now bothered to depilate – Sally herself was a rare exception. It was one of the many things that were too much trouble.

Sally thought of the hairless fireman, this hairless girl. The hairy Hobley and the hairy Arleen. And the vast majority of ordinary people, neither as hairless as one couple nor as hairy as the other.

Almost like three different races.

Practically, she wondered most why in nineteen years the matter had never brought itself to her attention and now within twenty-four hours it banged on the door of her awareness, impossible to ignore, whether it turned out to be really important or not. But of course it was not really new, it was simply something that made you think *I must have been mistaken* until at last you couldn't say it any more, knowing you were not mistaken.

She couldn't be mistaken about Arleen.

This girl had hair only on her head and even there it was not thick, clinging closely to her head like a black bathing cap. Elsewhere where she might have had hair she was not faintly blue but as pale and smooth as a baby – or as Conan Hersholt's chin.

At last the girl, poised for another dive, did sense that there was somebody close by. She tensed and listened like a timid animal. That she had still not seen Sally was evident from the way she looked around the island, then at the river banks, before finally scanning the water and spotting Sally, who was making no attempt to hide.

Sally waved. The girl, not alarmed, partly reassured, raised an arm and made a vague gesture that nearly amounted to waving back. Then she dived in and swam upstream, away from Sally.

Sally started after her. She could have overhauled her easily. But then Sally was struck by a certain similarity to what had happened to her . . . Hobley had wanted to speak to her, while she wanted to be left alone. The girl had the same right.

So Sally turned lazily, made for the island and climbed up on it. The girl looked over her shoulder, saw Sally and stopped.

For a moment it looked as if she would swim back.

Sally was not sure why she had climbed out of the water and let the girl have a good look at her. Perhaps to show that she had nothing whatever with her, that she was young, female and naked, like the girl. Also to show that she was not going to chase her.

At first sight of Sally on the island, the girl nearly swam back . . . Sally, no genius but also no fool, was compelled to wonder if this was because the girl had seen that she, too, had no body hair. It didn't make much sense, yet it was the only thing Sally could think of that made any sense at all.

Anyway, the girl changed her mind. She smiled, she did wave, and then swam upstream.

Sally watched her round a bend in the river, then dived in and swam downstream. It was a strange encounter, stranger than the mere facts of it. The girl did not fear her, yet she did not want to meet her and talk to her.

There was an old, still widely-believed idea that hairiness in men implied virility and that warm, generous women had long, thick, luxuriant hair on their heads. There was the old symbolic legend of Samson. And wasn't this ancient feeling behind the custom of shaving the heads of women who had in some way sinned – trying to make them not-women?

Sally thought out for herself things like how to ensure regular supplies for her shops, whether to enter new fields and whether to employ another assistant, but when she wondered about something and there were people who must obviously know the answer, she seldom tried to work it out for herself. She went to them and asked them.

So when she got back she would ask Arleen. And she would go to the fire-station and ask Conan. Meantime she was very hungry.

Conan was on his way to call on Beverley Daley.

He had no car and the public transport of Sherburn was unreliable. You could spend forty minutes waiting for a bus and when it came, so did four others in convoy. The drivers did this deliberately. Only the first bus had to pick up passengers. The others just came along for the ride. The drivers took it in turns to work and take it easy.

So he walked to the wealthy city-center district where Mrs Daley lived. Presently, finding himself later than he expected, he ran. People stared at him, for nobody ran. Conan, who was used to being stared at, didn't care.

Sooner or later, he thought, both Normans and Saxons would have to take care to avoid being stared at.

It was interesting that the *Sherburn Weekly*, which had suddenly and unexpectedly come out that morning, reported the fire at the shop and the death from suffocation of Arleen Jones with such careful restraint. Some time he would have to find out who ran the paper. It was probably a Norman or a Saxon, and he couldn't tell which. Either would have treated the story with the same caution. But only a Norman or a Saxon would have rushed out a paper to say nothing in particular – to be negative, in fact.

He was still hurrying, though not running any more. Beverley Daley was nothing to him, not being a Norman or a Saxon, and he didn't expect to enjoy the meeting. But it was impossible not to see him. And punctuality could be important, sometimes vital. So many people nowadays used so many excuses . . . as good an excuse as any was *He didn't turn up, so I went out.* Or *She wasn't there, so I went home.*

He had to pass the huge Sherburn Plastics factory. A man called Gardner was the boss, some said almost the sole owner now, having gradually bought up pieces of the enterprise first for control and later so that all the profit would be his.

Conan barely glanced at the factory, but at the thought of Gardner, whom he didn't know, something stirred in his mind. Once when Gardner was mentioned, Anastasia suddenly went strangely non-committal.

Could it be that Arthur Gardner was the Beast?

Arthur Gardner, still feeling good, walked round his empire, surveying it.

The factory was big and untidy. Although it was called Sherburn Plastics and plastics were produced, the fuel section was now far more important than plastics. The hydrogenation plant produced most of England's light, oil, heavy oil, fuel oil and gasolene, as well as gas for heating and lighting in Sherburn itself.

There was still plenty of gas and oil under the North Sea, but the rigs were dying of old age and lack of repair facilities, and it was becoming very difficult to get men to work on them. So hydrogenation and Sherburn Plastics came into their own.

On the face of it the market was small and shrinking, since every year there were fewer engines running on oil or gasolene. But this didn't bother Sherburn Plastics, because every year there were fewer alternative sources of supply. Gardner was considering manufacturing engines in a year or two to use his own fuel. He could do it, too: his factory was one of the few remaining on Earth which could tackle such a project and make it profitable. He was waiting, however, until Sherburn Plastics was the *only* factory which could do it successfully. Some engines would always be needed. With a monopoly he could make them bigger, more fuel-consuming.

There was purpose in the factory, purpose lacking almost everywhere else. There was not, unfortunately, 100 per cent efficiency: that was no longer possible. Machines broke down, and though there was skill enough to repair them, there was no longer skill enough to make new and better machines.

Gardner, a realist, would have paid top men top wages. But he had only about a score of men and half a dozen women so good in their various lines that he could not afford to let them go. The hundreds of others were paid what he considered them worth, and they stayed because, low as this was, it was higher than they themselves considered they were worth.

Except Frank Seymour. Seymour, forty-seven, specialist molder, came up to Gardner and said: 'Mr Gardner, can I talk to you?'

Gardner said nothing. Anything he said could be used against him, so he waited.

And as Seymour spoke haltingly, Gardner thought not of the words but of what was behind them.

Seymour wasn't a bad worker, reliable though slow. Gardner knew all his useful men and Seymour was just useful enough to be known to him.

Seymour had a large family and an aggressive wife who pushed him, without much success. He might, on his own, have asked for more money, probably not, but he would never, on his own, have threatened to leave if he didn't get it.

Gardner was weighing the matter and deciding he would keep Seymour if he could, yet had no intention of paying him any more, when a marvellous, exciting prospect opened itself up to him.

'You have six children, I believe,' he said casually.

Brought up short, Seymour said uneasily, reluctantly: 'Seven, Mr Gardner.' Gardner meant, of course, that he couldn't walk out, didn't dare walk out. And he was right.

Gardner, in fact, was thinking nothing of the sort.

'Their names and ages, please,' he said.

Still more uneasily, Seymour said: 'Well, my eldest boy, Frankie, he's sixteen. Then there's Ethel, fourteen, and Gwen, thirteen. The twins, Joe and Jim, they're eleven. Harry is ten and Meg eight.'

It could not be better. A whole family, the oldest not too old and the youngest not too young. The Beast wallowed in bestial anticipation. Seven children in his power. One at a time – eventually, as a climax, all together. Seven children who must have a certain unity, a certain bond. He could even make them work on each other. A boy of sixteen with all a sixteen-year-old boy's aggressions and fears and shames. Two adolescent girls. Twins . . . what a rich field for experimentation they might prove to be. A ten-year-old boy and a girl of eight – the terror of a girl of eight would be something for a connoisseur. Yet she was not too young to remember her fear, to understand that she must keep certain things to herself.

First, however, he had to break Seymour completely. This had to be done by stages. You didn't get total control of a family merely by frightening the breadwinner a little, though that wasn't a bad start. The pressures had to be subtly built up at half a dozen different points. Vince would have to help.

Vince, he realized in a moment of insight, was going to be a willing, even enthusiastic partner in this, not to please or satisfy him, but because the basic cruelty of it would appeal to him.

A family dehumanized. A family ground to dust.

'Very well, Seymour,' he said indifferently. 'Sorry to lose you, and all that. But if you feel you can do better elsewhere, I'm not going to stop you.'

From the sheer terror in the man's eyes he knew he could not have done better if he had had hours to prepare and practice his speech.

'Pity, though,' he added thoughtfully. 'I haven't used you in design, though I know that's your field, because every layabout wants to get into design and vacancies are scarce. But in a matter of weeks there's going to be a top job going in design ...'

Terror, then hope. He had thrown a non-swimmer into deep water and then cast him a line.

'I didn't know about that, sir,' Seymour gasped. He had never called Gardner 'sir' before, just 'Mr Gardner'. 'If there's a possibility ... if staying on would give me a chance – '

'May be months,' said Gardner, pulling in the line without Seymour on it. 'I'm going to move Foster, I tell you that in confidence. So I'm going to need a new head of design, but when ...'

Seymour swallowed. 'Mr Gardner, couldn't we just forget what I said?'

'Well now, what's said can never be quite forgotten. And I'm glad to hear you're ambitious, Seymour, that you want to get on, even if it's not with us.' He nearly asked where Seymour had planned to go, but that would expose him, and Gardner didn't want to expose him. Instead he said: 'Tell you what – I could put you in design now, at a lower salary for the time being, and you can get the hang of things. Then maybe later – '

Seymour closed with the offer eagerly and Gardner nodded and passed on, outwardly calm, inwardly gleeful. He had not only set up Seymour for the pressures to come, he had answered a demand for more money by giving him less and left Seymour uneasily grateful for it.

This put him in such a pleasant frame of mind that when Vince phoned him and told him guardedly of his total failure with the girl Sally Wells, instead of snarling at him Gardner told him tolerantly it didn't matter and he could forget the girl.

A mature, determined, uncooperative girl was not to be compared, for the delights he now had in mind, with eight-year-old Meg Seymour.

'I must see him alone, Mrs Daley,' Conan insisted.

She was jealous of any human contact with her precious Beverley, that was obvious. If she could, she would have kept him entirely to herself. She, not Beverley, was the real psychopath, Conan thought.

He was not so sure when he met Beverley, lying limp on a sunlounger in the wilderness at the back of the house.

Mrs Daley had been right in one respect. Beverley was beautiful. He had wavy golden hair and his thinness of face and body merely sharpened his beauty. Conan was reminded of certain statues of Greek gods created by decadent sculptors who, in their search for ultimate masculine beauty, had turned to women for their inspiration and lovingly carved naked bodies which were wholly masculine yet smooth, soft, hairless, with a delicacy of feature and muscle that no red-blooded male had ever possessed.

The paradox was that Beverley, despite his looks and all that Conan had heard about him from Anastasia, despite all that he was consciously or unconsciously inflicting on himself, was not effeminate. Indeed, Conan sensed his essential masculinity at the same moment as he sensed the elan that explained it, the elan that meant Beverley was a Norman.

A hung-up Norman, of course. That happened. Conan guessed Arleen Jones had been a hung-up Saxon. Beverley was denying everything, denying his masculinity, denying he was a Norman (that was easy, since he had probably never heard the word), denying himself most of all.

'I'm Conan Hersholt.'

Beverley didn't even look at him. Understandable – Beverley was denying his existence too.

'I've come to see you.' That was deliberately obvious. Conan had to get some sort of response. 'And it was worth it. I've never seen anybody quite like you.'

Flattery got him nowhere.

Shock tactics. 'You're dying of thirst, do you know that?'

A flicker of reaction this time: Beverley at least looked at him. Then he looked down at the ground, and Conan realized that the large bottle of bright red liquid, more than half empty, must be the one Anastasia had given Mrs Daley. Evidently Anastasia's idea had worked to some extent. Beverley had drunk enough of it to effect a considerable improvement in his fluid-intake situation. As of this moment he was not dying of thirst, he was on the way back. Probably he had taken only a sip at first, then more as his parched body demanded more and gradually became more capable of handling it. . .

Beverley moved only his right arm. It came up with his hand grasping the bottle neck, slowly and painfully, as if even that was an effort, and then with sudden, surprising strength dashed the bottle on a stone wall nearby, smashing it.

The red liquid momentarily shone on the green grass, then drained away into the soil.

That was something, Conan thought. For the first time he had got through.

'So you didn't know.'

Beverley closed his eyes.

If there was one thing with which Conan was well supplied it was patience. Not knowing even that he was trying to commit suicide, Beverley could not possibly know that he was a Norman.

'Beverley, you're a Norman. Have you heard the word?'

Conan expected no reaction to this, but surprisingly he got one.

'Newman?' Beverley said.

'Newman, that's right. We used to call ourselves Newman. A couple of years ago, with 2066 coming up, somebody said something about the Newman Conquest. Soon it became the new Norman Conquest. And Newman became Normans. At the same time Sexons became Saxons. I don't know whether we called them that or they started calling themselves that, trying to suggest they were the real inheritors of the country and we were the usurpers – '

His eyes still closed, Beverley said: 'Go away.'

'Beverley, you're sick. Mentally and physically. It's not entirely your fault – I know about your mother. She loves you, but what she's doing to you is – '

'My mother loves only her cats.' Beverley opened his eyes, and then closed them again.

Conan was prepared to talk with him about anything, anything at all. 'Cats? I haven't seen any cats.'

'They're not here. She has another house, just for her cats. She spends more time with them than with me.'

This was interesting. The pattern was becoming clearer. Mrs Daley had no husband, no natural outlet for her emotions. She had a son whom she loved unnaturally, and she had cats. Conan didn't need to ask how many cats. There must be a multitude of cats. And she kept a house for them.

'Your mother loves you all right,' Conan said carefully. 'And she's trying to help you. But she's helping you the wrong way. This nonsense about letting yourself die has got to stop. Drink, man, drink! Here, take a pull of this.'

Curiosity was not dead in Beverley. He had to open his eyes to see what he was being invited to drink. And as he opened them, Conan reached out with the flask.

It was less trouble for Beverley to take it than refuse it. He unscrewed the top and took a long pull. He was, naturally, torn many ways. His neurosis (if that was it) commanded him not to drink, while his body thirsted. Some complicated rationalization had allowed him to drink a good deal of Anastasia's bottle which was supposed to be medicine.

Now as he took the flask he thirsted and allowed himself to drink. That the liquid burned his mouth and throat was no reason to stop drinking it . . . if it was acid or poison, so much the better. He felt the burning in his mouth, throat, gullet and belly, the warmth, and he welcomed life or death, not caring which.

'Remarkable,' said Conan, dazedly accepting the empty flask. He had made the brandy himself. Doubts might be expressed about its quality (he had none), but there could be no doubt about its strength.

'So I'm a Norman,' said Beverley, his voice already stronger and deeper. He was not intoxicated. The alcohol had not yet reached his bloodstream, far less his brain. But he was afire, tingling all over, and he was not dying – not that he cared, for if this was death he should have tried it long ago – but suddenly alive in every pore. He looked at his visitor with interest for the first time.

'You're very thin on top,' he observed.

'And you're not,' said Conan, seizing the opportunity. 'Do you have hair on your chest too?'

Already that bombshell of neat alcohol was spreading through Beverley Daley. He sat up, marvelling at his own strength, and pulled his tunic apart. He was as hairless as an egg. It was confirmation which Conan did not need.

'What *was* that stuff?'

'Brandy.'

'I've never heard of it.'

Not surprising. He had never had alcohol in his life, not beer, cider or wine, and then, thirsty, he emptied a flask of brandy.

Suddenly Conan liked him. Liking between Normans came quickly if it came at all. And it more or less had to be mutual.

'What was that you said?' Beverley asked, his speech already becoming slurred. 'About me dying of thirst?'

'Many people these days have the death wish. Sometimes it's conscious, sometimes unconscious. Yours was unconscious. Something made you deny yourself enough water.'

'I'm thirsty now. Have you any more of that stuff?'

'No, and you can't take any more. It wouldn't quench your thirst, it would make you thirstier.'

'Why?'

Conan didn't want to get bogged down in an explanation of the effects of alcohol. 'You know it burns. Water will put out the fire. Water, tea, milk, coffee, anything.'

'I don't want to put out the fire.' Still sitting up, Beverley swung his legs out. The effort was too much. He lost his balance and nearly fell on his face.

Conan helped him back on the sunlounger. Dazed now, Beverley was more than willing to lie back. His eyes flickered.

'That's all right,' Conan said encouragingly. 'You want to sleep. Go ahead. But listen to this first. When you awake, you'll have a headache and a raging thirst. You'll want to drink. So drink. Drink all you want. I'll come back and see you.'

But already Beverley was flat out. Conan looked down at him thoughtfully.

Beverley would sleep for hours, three or four at least. There was no point in staying.

'Well?' said Mrs Daley anxiously, as he tried to pass her on his way out.

'He's all right. Sleeping.' Conan hesitated. What should he tell her? Finally he said: 'Mrs Daley, if you love your son – '

'If I love Beverley?' she interrupted incredulously.

'If you love him, you'll encourage him to go out, meet people, get to know girls. If he doesn't do that, he'll die.'

She struggled to understand.

Conan pretended more indifference than he felt. 'It's up to you. Do you want him dead on your terms or alive on his?'

While she was still pondering that, he brushed past her and went out.

After an early but satisfying meal at the farm, and a deal for mutton on the side, Sally cycled back to Sherburn and her responsibilities. She didn't phone the Cornwall Place shop, she cycled straight there. The fact that it was locked did not greatly surprise her. Arleen no doubt fancied herself ill, possibly *was* ill following the shock of David's death.

A woman passing said: 'You're Sally Wells, aren't you? Don't you know?'

'Don't I know what?'

It was not until then, nearly twenty-four hours after it happened, that she heard about the fire and Arleen's suicide. She felt irritation and frustration rather than sorrow and sympathy. If Arleen and David had really loved each other, at least Arleen's suicide would have made some sort of sense. But Arleen had lost only what she never had.

Practically, Sally gave Arleen a good mark for shutting up the shop instead of using it for her funeral pyre, as she might well have done.

Sally ran up the stairs to the top flat and found it empty and not badly damaged. The roof was not affected and that was what mattered. The shop wouldn't have to stay closed. She ran downstairs, cycled round to the other shop and sent one of the two girls there round to open the Cornwall Place store.

Then she went to the fire station. There was nobody there but a plump girl with a sniff and a face twitch.

'Conan Hersholt?' said the girl, and looked at Sally suspiciously, jealously. 'No, he's not here.'

Sally didn't have to be told that the girl had a personal interest in Conan. Was it possible that it was mutual?

'When will he be here?'

'At noon,' said the girl reluctantly. That was less than fifteen minutes away.

'I'll wait.'

'You can't wait here. Besides, he'll be on duty. Busy. I have three calls already for him to make.'

It was no surprise to Sally that fire calls, presumably emergency calls, had to wait for a single fireman to turn up.

'Then I'll wait outside,' she said.

The fire station was an imposing sandstone building with four big doors opening onto a main street. One of the doors was open, and a small red van, possibly the one Conan had used the day before, stood in a bay intended for a huge fire engine with a ladder and hoses.

Directly opposite was a café with two gaily-umbrellaed tables set outside. Sally wheeled her bicycle across and ordered lemonade.

'No lemonade,' said the elderly shopkeeper – he was not a waiter, obviously the owner. He eyed her bare legs with disfavor, wanting to refuse to serve her but afraid she would make a scene.

Sally propped her bicycle against one of the tables, sat down and said: 'Well, tea, then.'

'No tea.'

'You must have something,' she said reasonably, smiling up at him. The smile failed to charm him. He didn't know that he disliked her because she stirred him, and disapproved of her skimpy sweater and shorts because she was young and well-formed and he was old and fat.

'Beer,' he said reluctantly.

'Beer?' She was surprised, but nodded. 'All right. Beer.'

The café was not licensed and he was breaking the law by selling beer. But she was surprised at herself for being surprised – every month there was less law. A café proprietor who couldn't get lemonade or tea or coffee and could get beer would naturally take it in and sell it. The chances of prosecution were remote.

Tea had to come from India, coffee from South America. Supplies were not exactly scarce, just unreliable. Middlemen would offer a dealer half a ton of tea, not less, simplifying delivery. A café like this wouldn't get through half a ton of tea in ten years.

Sally could supply tea and coffee. It would be good business to do so even at a loss, for too many shops and cafés were closing. And why not take a leaf out of the café proprietor's book and sell beer in the shops? Beer was made locally from English malted barley and Kent hops.

Sally had no ambition to be very rich, but she liked efficiency. In a couple of years she could have a dozen shops. The only difficulties were getting reliable staff and establishing further sources of supply.

She had scarcely started on the frothy brown pint when she saw Conan across the street, making for the fire station.

She rang the bell of her cycle loudly, and he turned, saw her, and trotted across the street.

'What a pleasant surprise,' he said mildly. 'It's Miss Wells.'

'Sally.'

'Miss Wells yesterday. Sally today?'

'I know you now. Today, if you still wanted to kiss me, maybe you could.'

'Tomorrow?'

She grinned. 'Want a beer?'

'I have to go and work.'

'I know. There are three calls for you.'

'You know about Arleen Jones?'

'Not until a few minutes ago. Why, were you – it wasn't you who was at the fire?'

There was too much to talk about. 'Look – how about coming with me? You can put your bike in the back of the van again.'

'That was my idea too.' She picked up the beer and killed it in one long, practised swallow. Despite the fact that she was clearly no stranger to beer, or brandy for that matter, it wasn't possible that she drank a lot, Conan thought, catching a brief glimpse of a taut brown midriff as she threw her head back.

Still no elan. But the aura was stronger, better defined.

Once there had been a thing called personality. A girl with personality didn't need beauty. But a girl with beauty and personality was really something.

Now there was scarcely anybody with personality. No peasant had it – it was a contradiction in terms. No Normans had it, Normans generally being quiet, self-effacing, well balanced (if they weren't hung up like Beverley Daley). Only Saxons sometimes had personality, like Meredith Dundee and a few others – not all Saxons had it by any means.

Sally's aura was not quite what used to be called personality, but it was very like it.

You couldn't ignore her.

She glowed.

The first call was to a smoldering rubbish dump. It didn't particularly matter. The more rubbish that burned the better. Garbage collection was one of thousands of things nearing the point of breakdown.

They talked guardedly about Arleen, David, the fires, bringing themselves up to date but without embarking on anything new and important.

The second fire was a blazing hut near a house – and nobody had bothered to remove a line of combustible rubbish between them which would shortly have set the house on fire. Sally helped, working with strength, vigor and a sturdy common sense which, Conan decided, was perhaps the most characteristic thing about her.

The third was a hoax call. And Sally for the first time saw Conan angry.

'There's so little we can do,' he said. 'We're short of everything, most of all men and time. A hoax call can mean that lives which could have been saved are not.'

'How much does the job pay?' she asked, not irrelevantly.

'A hundred a week.'

'That all? Why do you do it?'

'It has to be done.'

'I'll give you two hundred to work for me.'

'You could pay me two hundred pounds a week? Guaranteed?'

'Certainly.'

'Shops are always closing down. Businesses are going bust.'

'Businesses are being allowed to go bust. Not mine. You'd have to work.'

'I work now.'

'I know.'

'I'm doing a useful job.'

'Is putting out fires any more important than feeding people?'

'Perhaps not,' he admitted.

'Meantime I want you to tell me something.'

The van had no radio. He turned off the road at a phone-box, got out and called the fire station for instructions. Surprisingly, there were no more alerts. He gave the number of the kiosk, propped the door open with a stone, and went back to sit with Sally in the van.

'Well?' he said.

She touched his face. Round his mouth, under his chin, the skin was no different from the skin on his cheekbones or on his temples.

Her hand slid into the open neck of his shirt, over his smooth chest to his armpit. It was as smooth as his face.

'Try lower down,' he invited. 'I'm not shy.'

'No. Then you'd want to do the same to me. There's no need. I'll tell you. I don't have fur growing all over me. And I'm not as hairless as you. What does it mean?'

'That,' he said carefully, 'everybody has to find out for himself.'

'There are three different kind of people. Hairless. Nearly hairless. Furry. You. Me. Arleen.'

'Norman, peasant, Saxon. I'll give you that free.'

'And does it matter?'

'Yes.'

'Arleen. Saxon. She knew things. Clairvoyance, telepathy, something like that. And you're a Norman. What tricks can you do?'

He stayed silent. If she had been a Norman, even a Saxon, he could have told her all he knew, which was not much. But she was not a Norman . . . that lovely thick hair on her head meant he and she could never be everything to each other. They could make love, of course – it was the duty of every Norman and Saxon to reproduce as copiously as possible, so that their race would inherit the Earth.

He remembered his sudden strange certainty that he and Sally would never make love, and it still puzzled him. He sensed Sally's distrust of impulse – it was in her aura, a refusal to be rushed, a determination to look before she leaped – and at the same time he sensed that she had no strong ties and was perfectly willing to make love to him when she knew him better.

But there was a new snag . . . and that showed in her aura too. Annoyance, irritation that he had told her so little and seemed to have no intention of telling her more was putting up a barrier between them.

'Tricks,' he said. 'All right. I'll show you a couple. Here's one.'

He started the motor and leaned back, touching nothing. The engine ran, then faltered, then stopped.

Beside him, her hip touching his, she could see and feel that he had not moved either hands or feet. 'You're not telling me you did that?'

'Have you a watch?'

'Obviously I haven't got a watch.'

'Take mine. Hold it so I can see it too.'

He turned the key and started the engine again. 'It will run,' he said, 'for exactly two minutes. Then it'll stop.'

She knew this time, when the motor stopped, that he wouldn't have gone to the trouble of faking such a demonstration. 'How?' she asked simply.

'It's only a very small miracle. Engines often stall. The mixture is momentarily too rich, the spark weak. Any one of a dozen things can happen.'

He shrugged and smiled. 'I just make any one of them happen, and I don't even know which.'

'Start it without touching it.'

His grin became wider. 'Now there you have me. I told you it was only a very small miracle. Starting the motor's too big for me. Oh, I've managed to do it, but only once in a hundred tries. I can't turn over the starting motor, not with the key where it is. And the dead engine, though the ignition is still on, can't suck in gas and air. And the points are held so that they can't spark. The few times I've been successful, I suppose it just happened to be possible to tip the rotor arm a fraction of an inch so that there was a spark, and induce the mixture to ignite, and the motor started. Normally though . . . wait a moment.'

He pondered, 'It might be possible to stop the motor in such a way, at such a position, that when I wanted to I could cause a spark and . . . anyway, let's try.'

He started the motor again. As before, it faltered and died. Ten seconds later, of its own volition, it started again.

As he reached for the key and switched off, Sally said: 'What good is it?'

'Not much,' he said apologetically. 'You asked for a trick.'

'Well, I can't see that saving your life or mine.'

'Neither can I. But since you mention it – if somebody shot at me, or you for that matter, and I saw him and the gun in time, neither of us would have a scratch.'

Sally sat up, turning to stare at him. 'That's different.'

'It is, isn't it?'

'How would you do that?'

He shrugged. 'Same way, I can't do the impossible any more than anybody else. Something that could happen I just help along a little, that's all.'

'You said a couple of tricks. What's the other?'

He moved an inch or two away so they were not touching. Nothing happened.

Then something did happen. Sally sat bolt upright, her cheeks going pink.

'I didn't touch you,' he insisted.

'I know you didn't . . . ' She was momentarily embarrassed and self-conscious, a thing which rarely happened to her. With a man's hands on her body, caressing her, rousing her, she might not be able to stop him turning her on – but then, she could always slap a man's hands.

You couldn't slap a man's hands when he had ostentatiously put them in his pockets.

'Stop it,' she said crossly.

'I already have.'

But her own impulses had taken over. She wanted sex. Only stubbornness, an obstinate refusal to be manipulated, made her refuse to give in to the impulse and to Conan.

The bell in the callbox started to ring, and Conan got out to take the call.

He was soon back. 'Take an hour off, they told me,' he said wryly. 'Nothing doing just now. And stay an hour later at night.'

'Are you going to work for me?'

'Maybe.' Perhaps nature had a few more tricks up her sleeve, like a new, superior grade of peasant. Certainly he had nothing to lose by staying in contact with Sally.

He made up his mind. 'Sally, how about coming with me to see somebody?'

Vince, his wrist strapped, was not as imperturbable as usual. He was in a cold rage, and Gardner enjoyed it. It was amusing to think of the girl getting the better of Vince. Gardner enjoyed it the more because there was no need for him to feel involved in Vince's failure. Gardner had not failed with Sally Wells; Vince had.

In his rage Vince did not enter into Gardner's plans for the Seymour family as otherwise he might have done. Yet he displayed grudging interest. Gardner and Vince both took a certain vicarious interest in the plans of the other, Gardner in Vince's revenge on Sally Wells and Vince in Gardner's campaign against a whole family.

The main thing the two men had in common was that they were both conscious, deliberate diabolists. They enjoyed evil for its own sake.

'Of course it will be much simpler for me than you, Mr Gardner,' Vince said, unable to resist sniping. 'Frankly, I can't see you being successful. While in my case I can't see anything else . . . You can frighten Seymour, control him maybe, but how can that put the whole family in your hands?'

'There will be a way,' said Gardner. 'To find it I need your help. Your damaged wrist won't be a handicap. At first I merely want to find out about the Seymours, from Frank and Margaret down to young Meg.'

'Money?'

'All you want.'

'Help? Men, women?'

'No. This has to be discreet. I trust no one but you.'

That was a laugh. Some day, when the time was right, Vince had every intention of destroying Gardner, when he would gain more than he would lose by doing so.

And Gardner knew all about that.

On the way Conan told Sally a little about Beverley Daley. She found little to surprise her in the idea of a man thirsting to death, since from birth she had lived with suicide although she had never had the urge to get into the act.

The idea of a man cut off from women all his life was more strange to her, since in the nature of things she could scarcely have met such a man.

'What do you want me to do?' she asked.

'That depends. Maybe he'll scream at the sight of you. Or try to kill you.'

'That'll be nice.'

'I'll be there. And you can look after yourself, can't you?'

'Oh yes. But twice in one day seems too much.'

Questioned, she told him about Hobley. When she saw him becoming interested in Hobley she said: 'Yes, he's a Saxon.'

'You do know about them. You've encountered them before?'

'Hairy men. Not hairless ones.'

'You're about to meet one of the others.'

'And he's trying to kill himself unpleasantly by not drinking? I thought Normans were supposed to be some superior kind of being. The race of the future to replace us apes?'

He realized, as evidently she did too, that if they talked at all her curiosity was going to be satisfied gradually, even if he never let her fire questions at him and answered them all.

'Latents can be hung up. I thought you could be a latent.'

'But I can't be because I'm not bald?'

'That's not conclusive.' He hesitated, but did not tell her about the elan she lacked, which proved she was no Norman, or the remarkable aura she possessed, which almost proved she was no peasant. It hung about her now like a golden radiance, gilding the lily . . . she was attractive enough without it, with her bare legs and arms, explicit sweater and nearly as explicit shorts. He realized that the ancient concept of saints with a halo must have come from some hazy perception of the aura of great men long ago. Artists with the inner eye had painted it clumsily, prosaically. Although they failed miserably to get across what they had seen, they proved beyond doubt that they had seen something.

Sensing that there was something he was not telling her, Sally did not tell him about the girl she had seen that morning.

When they reached the Daley house, it seemed their luck was in. A frozen-faced housekeeper opened the door, and though she looked with scant approval at Conan and at Sally with less, she stood aside to let them come in. Then, without a word, she closed the door, pointed up the stairs, and returned to the back of the house.

'It seems Mrs Daley had to go out,' said Conan, leading the way upstairs. 'The cats, of course. Mrs Daley's cats may turn out to be useful. But for them she'd be standing guard on Beverley twenty-four hours a day . . . Wait here, Sally.'

He found Beverley in an overheated, underventilated, over-decorated room, lying on a divan, but awake. He groaned at sight of Conan, yet his eyes lighted up a little.

'I know,' said Conan sympathetically, taking note of the coffee-pot and cup on a table beside the divan. 'Next time you will too. You don't drink brandy like that.'

'I'll never drink it again,' said Beverley hoarsely. He was sweating, not surprisingly in the heat of the room. He threw off a heavy sweater, unbuttoned his shirt, and then, with an impatient gesture, pulled off the shirt too.

It was interesting to confirm that his body was wholly hairless. He wore only blue hipster jeans, belted low across his hips. His pale, streaming body, though so thin that every rib showed, was in better shape than Conan expected. Saxons and Normans tended to be stronger physically than the peasants – perhaps a reflection of the importance of sexual drive in human beings. Its weakening or loss tended to hasten physical dissolution in other respects. It had been Sally's glowing health and obvious capacity for sex that first made Conan hope he had discovered a true Norman in her.

'Like many things,' Conan said, 'brandy is good in small doses, bad in excess. Have you heard the expression "hair of the dog"?'

'Yes. What does it mean?'

Conan produced the refilled flask. Beverley looked at it with the fascination of a trapped animal.

'Take my word for it,' said Conan, 'a small pull will do you good. But only a little.'

Beverley reached for the flask. He drank deeply, too deeply, and Conan snatched it from him. 'Careful,' he warned. 'Moderation, remember.'

'In some ways I don't feel too bad,' Beverley said, surprisingly. Unconsciously he touched his smooth chest, his flat belly – narcissism? It might well be that a mixed-up but virile man, denied women and probably totally ignorant of homosexuality, had nowhere to turn but narcissism.

It seemed a good moment to observe Sally's effect on Beverley. Not raising his voice, he said: 'Come in.'

Sally came in. Conan saw her only out of the corner of his eye, for he was observing Beverley closely.

What happened was unexpected. Beverley tried to hide himself, curling up, making a grab for his shirt and sweater. Missing them and knocking them on the floor, he used his arms to try to cover himself, not his genitals, which were covered anyway, but his naked navel, his bare chest.

'Think nothing of it, Mr Daley,' said Sally. 'I don't care if you don't wear a tie.'

Behind the couch, Conan beckoned Sally, and she moved closer to Beverley. There might be sexier garments than her sweater and shorts, but Conan doubted it. She would look more elegant but less vital in a glamorous dress.

'No,' said Beverley. 'Don't come any closer.' Yet he was more relaxed, curious now rather than alarmed.

That was another proof that he was a Norman. A few hours ago he had been as mixed-up as any Saxon. But the effects of shaking him up had all been good. He didn't resent Conan, even seemed quite glad to see him again. Since the warning about what he had not consciously known, that he was inflicting thirst on himself, he had drunk copiously. And though the introduction of Sally had been a shock, it seemed to be a shock from which he could rapidly recover.

Conan mimed talking and pointed down at Beverley.

'You must have seen plenty of girls,' he said.

'No. I hardly ever go out.'

'Then it's time you did. How about us all going out now?'

He hesitated, then shook his head. Then he turned his head away.

The withdrawal, just when Conan had been thinking with satisfaction that since he met him Beverley had shown few of the expected signs of withdrawal, was a disappointment. Wondering whether to go along with it or to fight it, Conan caught Sally's eye and saw she was wondering the same thing.

Characteristically she decided to fight it. She moved forward to sit on the divan beside Beverley's legs. Seeing the movement, he turned back and his earlier terror returned. He tried to draw away, even swung his legs out on the other side as if to run from her – and then, as he had done that morning (but then under the influence of a full flask of brandy) lost his balance and righted himself only with a considerable effort.

'Sally,' Conan said quietly, 'wait outside.'

He helped Beverley back onto the divan. 'Something wrong with your legs?' he said.

'They've always been weak.'

'But you were in the garden at the back. Now you're up here. How did you get here?'

'They carried me. They always do.'

'Let me see.' He rolled up Beverley's jeans. There seemed nothing wrong with them. The muscles were thin and weak, but there was no wasting.

'You can stand up?'

'Oh, yes. I can walk. I'm not a cripple. But mum doesn't like me to walk. She's afraid I'll fall. I *have* fallen, quite often.'

From birth Mrs Daley had coddled and cosseted her wonderful Beverley. She had not wanted him to walk too soon . . . probably she had been in no hurry for him to be housebroken either. And when he did walk, a few of the inevitable falls and minor injuries had made her fearful – and at the same time, perhaps, aware even then that if she could keep him relatively immobile she might keep him for life.

Keeping girls from him was much easier and more complete, of course, if he seldom went out. Two hundred years ago, when parents had total control of their children, this kind of thing might have happened. A hundred years ago it would have been quite impossible, for busy, bustling social services would have known all about the boy and if there was anything abnormal about him or his mother or the background there would have been visits by health visitors, social workers, doctors, psychiatrists, police, school attendance officers and scores of others. Now it was possible again – with hardly any social workers, doctors who never went near their patients, few and overworked police, and schools trying to unload pupils elsewhere, not add to their rolls.

'Beverley,' he said firmly, 'you've got to get out of here.'

But that, he knew as he said it, was going too far, too fast. Beverley couldn't think of leaving his home and his mum. First he had to get around to thinking it before he could do it.

'Don't call me Beverley. She always does. I'm Bev.'

'All right, Bev. You're going to be strong. You have a fine body, a beautiful body. For the first time in your life you're going to use it – take pleasure in it.'

Once again Bev's long fingers lightly touched his smooth flesh, probed delicately, and under his touch soft muscles moved.

Conan strode to the window and opened it. 'Come here, Bev.'

Falteringly Bev got up and walked slowly, carefully, to the window.

'The air,' Conan said. 'The clean air. Fill your chest with it. Stand straight like a man.'

The words were not important. He was doing more than speak to Bev. Elan reached out to elan, even if Bev didn't know it.

'Yes,' Bev said, suddenly excited. 'Now go away, please. Come back – yes, please come back – but just now, let me try for myself.'

Conan nodded. It was possible he had already done all Bev needed.

Left alone, Bev breathed deeply at the open window for a while – the air was fresher than it had been for centuries – and then started to do knee-bends.

He managed three.

3

For some days Sally was busy putting her business affairs in order. Her father had left the shops to David, not her, and though David had left her to run them and insisted that her name, not his, should go above the door, everything remained in his name and Sally had to shake up quite a few people before it was officially recognized that she was the new owner.

Then she had to call on all her suppliers and light fires under them, find three new assistants and train them. She found that David had been more useful than she had believed – after all he had nearly always done what she told him to do, eventually.

When Conan turned down her offer of a job she stopped seeing him, shrewdly aware that he had several kinds of interest in her and didn't want to lose contact with her. And when he turned up again she took him to the riverside spot where she had had her encounter with Hobley. She told Conan about Hobley, the Saxon, and the shy, dark girl, not pressing for information but acquiring a little more.

On the personal level she was maliciously reserved, trying to annoy him. She didn't swim, though he did, and kept the legs she knew he admired wrapped up in slacks.

'Why won't you work for me?' she demanded.

'I can't. I'm needed where I am. You don't need me.'

'Believe me, I do.'

He shook his head. 'You want me. You don't need me.'

'You're wasted putting out fires.'

'I know. But somebody's got to do it.'

At such moments, exasperated, she felt that his obstinacy

had something in common with the ineffective stubbornness of David. To her it was obstinacy, nothing more. He could have money, he could have a good and undeniably useful job, and he could very probably have her as well . . . but not one without the other.

For his part Conan was coming to realize that it didn't need the death of one of them to prevent his affair with Sally coming to its logical conclusion.

He could not work for her. He was a Norman. That carried certain obligations, as far as he was concerned. Saxons, he knew, used their semi-awareness and vital force to achieve wealth and power. Normans . . .

Sometimes Conan was not quite sure himself what being a Norman entailed.

'Have you seen Beverley Daley again?' Sally asked abruptly.

'Yes. Several times.'

'Well?'

'What do you want to know?'

'You took me to see him. You shouldn't have done that if you wanted to keep him one of your Norman secrets.'

'You've got the wrong idea, Sally.'

'Then why don't you put me right?'

'We're empaths,' he said simply.

'Empaths?'

'You've heard of telepaths. Neither Saxons nor Normans are telepaths. If they existed, there would be a meeting of minds. Among empaths, there's a meeting of feeling.'

'Love?'

'No. Not even understanding. That's mental – minds again. When empaths are together, each knows how the other feels. That doesn't mean each has to feel the way the other feels – '

Sally sniffed. 'We used to call that "atmosphere".'

'Yes, that's right. Empathy is nothing new . . . '

They went on like this for a while. Sally being in Conan's view, merely destructive, asking questions and then shooting down the answers.

The next day Conan returned to the same spot alone.

The following morning he was back again, and this time he was in luck. The dark girl came swimming downstream to the island, and Conan, hidden in the bushes, saw her climb out of the water. This time she wore a floral-patterned bikini and carried a waterproof plastic bag. Conan who was naked, reached for his swim trunks and pulled them on.

The girl sat on the warm sand, opened the bag, took out a pair of spectacles and a book, and put on the glasses.

Conan entered the water quietly and swam toward the island. The girl, reading her book, did not notice him until he climbed out of the water, less than ten steps from her. Then she jumped to her feet and turned to dive into the water.

'Wait,' said Conan quietly, with no fierceness or urgency in his tone. The girl paused. Their eyes met, but he couldn't see her very well behind her glasses. He stepped forward and she froze, realizing the uselessness of flight. He took off her glasses and their eyes met.

Her elan was like the first yellow-green shoot of a plant just breaking the soil. But it was there.

Undoubtedly, however, she knew nothing about what made her different from the peasants, even from Sally. Sally had the most powerful aura he had ever encountered, now that time had given him the chance to build up his perception of it, and this girl had none. But the baby elan made her more than Sally could ever be.

Slowly they sank to the ground, a yard apart.

'I'm Conan Hersholt.'

'Jan,' she said. 'Jan Callendar.' She was scared stiff. Now that he was close, he thought he could estimate her age more accurately than Sally had been able to do. A young sixteen, he decided. A woman, not a child, but a very inexperienced woman.

With or without her glasses she was very pretty. Not to be compared with Sally, of course, but it was not necessary to compare every girl with Sally, he thought, and then proceeded to do so. By coincidence they were both small, well shaped and pretty, but there the resemblance ended. Jan had dark, short, thin hair, and Conan realized with a slight shock that what he had once told Sally about hairless Normans finding hairlessness in others sexually attractive was not always true. Sally's thick blonde hair made hers the loveliest head he knew. Jan had all the usual curves but her body was soft where Sally's was hard, yielding despite her shyness where Sally's was a challenge.

Sally had thrown Hobley in the river and sprained his wrist. An eight-year-old boy could overcome this girl.

'Now there isn't the slightest need to be scared,' he said. 'I have to talk to you because of what you are. You know you're different from other people, don't you?'

'Different?' She was as scared as ever. 'No. How?'

'Oh. So you don't. Where do you live?'

'At Arley. A farm. It's quite near.'

'And what do you do?'

'Help in the house mostly. My father doesn't believe girls should work in the fields.'

'Your father owns the farm?'

'Yes.'

'What's he like?'

The question baffled her. He was her father. He wasn't like anything.

Yet she was less scared. Sensing her self-consciousness, he didn't look at her all the time as he spoke, turning back to her only now and then and never giving her a chance to think that he was staring at her.

'Different,' she said suddenly. 'Yes, I'm different. They're happy. I'm not.'

'They?'

'My mother and father. My three brothers.'

It was interesting, surprising, that she said her father, mother and brothers were happy and she was not. Could they be Normans too? The brothers might be, but not the parents. And if the brothers were Normans, Jan would not still be a latent.. So it must be as he had suspected from the first – Jan was a young latent Norman among peasants.

Yet why did her family seem happy to her? Who was happy these days except some children, some Normans, some Saxons, and Sally? How could even a latent Norman say her family was happy and she wasn't?

'Jan,' he said softly, 'you live on a farm. You must know all about how life goes on. Sex.'

Her fright returned. With it, however, was sudden wild interest. He knew he had found the right button, though he had no idea whether the right thing to do was press it or not.

'It's wrong, isn't it?'

'No, of course not.'

'I didn't think it was. Show me.'

It was not in the least surprising that she behaved like this, shy as she was. Words did not matter as much between Normans as between Norman and peasant, or between peasant and peasant. Nor did time. What mattered between Conan and Jan was empathy.

For centuries thinking men had taken it for granted that if ever a new race of supermen developed, intelligence would be paramount and emotion secondary.

They couldn't have been more wrong.

What happened between Conan and Jan was not animal, it was not promiscuous, it was inevitable. Neither a Norman nor a Saxon could be fully alive, fully aware, fully a Norman or a Saxon, while still a virgin. The girl's two strips of clothing dissolved between them and Conan, having ensured that no love play was necessary, entered her almost with his first touch. There was no pain and there was almost instant climax.

But of course the first consummation was only the start, a mere preliminary. The second embrace was more leisurely, yet still astonishingly rapid. The third time Conan began to need, and began to show, his experience in the arts of love, genuinely making love to Jan for the first time, teaching her, leading her as well as wooing her. The fourth was the first really beautiful act they shared, dramatic as even the first had been.

Then they lay naked in the warm sun, apart, and calmly looked at each other. And now the elan was mutual.

'There must have been real inspiration,' said the girl pensively, 'in that fairy tale invented so long ago. The princess awakened by the prince's kiss.'

He nodded. 'Symbolic, but a 100 per cent accurate. In your turn, Jan, you'll waken others.'

'Tell me about it.'

'I think probably the Sexons came first – about fifty years ago. As humanity surrendered to psychosis, boredom, frigidity, barrenness, impotence, the Sexons emerged – hairy, lustful, aggressive. The men were great lovers, the women wrongly regarded as nymphos. Most of their lovemaking was among themselves – for Sexons, like us, that's the most satisfying. An ordinary girl seldom – '

He explained the difference between her new experience and that of so many others. She listened in wonder.

'It was because of that,' he went on, 'that the Sexons christened the 99.99 per cent of the human race who weren't Sexon peasants. The Sexons despised them . . . but the peasants were to have their revenge. Despite the fact that sex with peasants was so dull and dead, the Sexons simply couldn't help indulging in it. The early Sexons didn't have any real control, they were forced to take sex as they took food and drink. They couldn't do without it. And at that time there was still law. Sexons were convicted of rape and sent to jail, and you might as well torture a Sexon to death as put him in jail.'

'I've never heard anything of this,' said the girl, frowning. 'Why not?'

'Because at first, when the Sexons were claiming to be a new race, nobody believed them. And almost at once the Sexons realized, individually and collectively, that instead of proving they were a new race they had to pretend they weren't, and hide in the crowd.'

'Why?'

'Sexons have no great gift except immense virility and an occasional clairvoyant ability. When Sexons were put in jail, new race or not, they had nothing to help them get out, Sexons outside couldn't help them, and numerically they were so few that they were helpless. Sexons realized they simply had to appear to toe the line, not to be identified, and not to be sent to jail.'

'What about the Normans?'

'We began to appear a little later, I think, but that may not be true because as a race we're less aggressive than the Sexons, more cautious, more in control of ourselves, more sympathetic, more responsible, and with all this, more secretive. Newmen, as we called ourselves at first, may have existed even before the Sexons, perhaps before the end of the twentieth century, but never drew attention to themselves. Newmen had the same sex drive as the Sexons, abnormal because among the peasants, though interest in sex stayed about the same as always, ability to do anything about it was dying.'

'And we're not hairy.'

'No.' He looked frankly now at her naked vulva, soft, smooth, pink, and could not imagine how so beautifully shaped a region of the female body had ever been considered 'dirty' and disgusting – so disgusting that the vernacular word for it was the most obscene of all the four letter words. Yet he realized – and this was significant – that if it had been covered with coarse hair he might have considered it 'dirty' and disgusting. Exposure of pubic hair had for long been a definition of obscenity in photographs sent by mail . . . he wondered, and did not know, whether that meant that a photograph of Jan exactly as she was now would not contravene the code.

Of course, Normans with their powerful sex drive were able to overlook the hairiness of peasants, even the hyperhairiness of Saxons, in sex. But Jan to him was far more beautiful than any naked peasant.

'Why do you think it happened?' Jan asked. 'I mean, the appearance of Sexons and Newmen more or less together?'

'When survival requires it, nature often provides two possible solutions at once, or six, or a score. They may not work. They may be evolutionary dead ends. Or they may all work. Nature doesn't mind conflict. Nature likes conflict. An all-out struggle for survival between Normans, Saxons and peasants would suit nature fine.'

'Do you have to call the people peasants?'

He smiled slightly. 'Give me another name and I won't.'

'How did the Newmen become Normans and the Sexons Saxons?'

He explained that.

'So the Normans and Saxons are at war?'

'No, not exactly. In fact no, not at all. We just don't get on, that's all. We can't even fight a secret war because it couldn't stay secret for long and the peasants, weak and indolent and indifferent as they are, might turn on us all.'

'If we're so different, so strong, would that matter?'

He shrugged. 'Lumping the Normans and the Saxons together, there's still two hundred peasants for every one of us.'

'Yet this is supposed to be the year of the Norman Conquest?'

'Jan, we didn't say that, it was wished on us by the Sexons – who started calling themselves Saxons at the same time and set themselves up as the true people, the native people, resisting the invader. The names that stick are often applied in contempt at first by the enemy – Methodists, Puritans, Contemptibles. That doesn't matter.'

'Then if there's no war, what do we *do*?'

'Become stronger.'

'How?'

'Nature's way. Reproduce ourselves. It's what we're meant to do, designed to do.'

'If you and I had a child, it would be a Norman?'

'Probably. Though it could be a peasant or even a Saxon which is one reason why we can't wage all-out war on the Saxons. We can't be sure we're not the same thing. But it isn't necessary for both parents to be Normans. The Norman and Saxon strains are dominant. A child of mine by a peasant is likely to be a Norman.'

'And no doubt you've had many?'

'Very many.'

'And how many are Normans?'

'I don't know. Because we don't develop until about eighteen or nineteen. Sometimes later.'

'So I'm not developed?'

'Now you are. Sex to us really is what the romantic writers of long ago tried to make it out to be.'

She nodded, not disposed to argue. She knew from her experience of the last hour or so that what he was saying was true.

'What usually happens,' he went on, 'is that a child Norman grows up just like a peasant child, but more serenely. Puberty at the usual time, no earlier. The fact that hair doesn't develop sometimes causes emotional and social problems . . . you should know about that.'

'No problem for me. Brothers, no sisters. I've always had a room of my own.'

'The twelve or thirteen-year-old mature Norman – or Saxon – pretty well has to get sexual experience. How did you manage to last out three years?'

Her answer was not in words. She looked at him, and he knew she had to have him again. He was ready and willing, and being a Norman he was always able.

Beverley swung his legs out of bed, did a knees bend and came up easily.

It might be tonight, or he might wait another night, another week.

First he locked his bedroom door, as he always did in the evening. His mother and the housekeeper were both heavy sleepers – it was this which had made him gradually reverse his routine, sleeping by day and waking up at night. Twice he had let Conan Hersholt in and they had talked . . .

Conan had nothing to do with his great resolution, however. Beverley had not let him have anything to do with it.

Conan had talked of sex often until Bev made him promise to drop the subject. Bev was still uneasy about girls and was glad Sally had never returned, even as he spent hours trying to remember every detail of her face, her clothes.

Bev stripped to black bathing briefs and switched out the light. He ran through the exercise routine he had developed, joying in the fact that he could do so much more than a week ago, more even than yesterday. He could wait for everything else, but he could not wait to be as strong as Conan, or stronger. Night after night he had driven himself more fiercely than any slavemaster, bending , stretching, lifting, running on the spot, straining. Always in the dark. Twice his mother had got up, twice he had waited concealed until she went back to bed.

At first he had been cold in slacks and sweater, but now he was not cold in bathing trunks. After a few minutes of the hard labor he imposed on himself he was bathed in sweat.

He knew there was something unnatural in his pleasure in his lean, pale, hairless body, but ignored that for the moment. This was a time of change. Even unnatural pleasure in the body which had never brought him pleasure before could be a stepping stone, and he spurned no stepping stones.

Throwing the window wide, he breathed the cool night air deeply. And two breaths did it.

Tonight he was going out. Alone. Now.

The night was moonless, but it was still an hour to midnight and there would be people about. He could not, however, bear the thought of putting on clothes. He wanted to walk, run, climb fences, walls and trees, and he wanted the cool night air on his bare skin. Reluctantly he put on soft plastic shoes, for his feet were not hard enough for him to go barefoot, but he put on nothing else.

There was nothing to stop him going out through the house, locking his bedroom door behind him so that if his mother checked she would think he was still there. The fact that he didn't answer meant nothing, since for more than a week now he had been answering her only when he felt like it, at the same time delighting her by eating and drinking as he had never done in his life before.

But sneaking out through the house was for some reason quite impossible. He didn't want to turn from that intoxicating clean night. And to go out alone for the first time in years, almost the first time in his life, would be no great adventure if he did so by the front door.

He climbed out of the window and tugged at the stout rope beside it. It was quite firm and he was sure it would support him. His hands and arms, unlike his legs, had always been strong, and lately he had been doing many exercises to strengthen them, like catching the top of open doors and pulling himself up by his arms to rest his chin on the top. He could lower himself to the ground by using his arms alone.

It was surprisingly easy to climb down to the ground, but Bev was not surprised. He could do far more than that, and he was going to.

There was, however, a moment of uneasiness as he climbed the high wall round the garden and realized that this was the last moment to draw back.

Then he was over the wall and running along the lane behind the house.

There was method in his madness, caution in his recklessness. He knew that the lane was almost certainly deserted, and at the end of it he merely had to cross one not-too-busy road to reach the park. And in less than two minutes he was up and over the railings and among the trees.

Inside the park, which was closed at ten, he found a tarmacadam path under his feet and started to run. Soon he was panting and his legs were rubbery, but he forced himself on and on in the gloom. He would not allow himself to stop, until he reached an open field in the middle of the park and the necessity to look carefully around him before venturing onto the field gave him an excuse to stop.

Despite the absence of a moon it was not pitch black here as it had been under the trees. Even there he had been able to stay on the path, and here, under the open sky, clear and lit by ten thousand stars, it would be possible to recognize a person three yards away.

Spontaneously Bev dropped to the damp grass and rolled over his head, not once but many times. Then he tried, at first unsuccessfully, to turn cartwheels. After a while he learned the trick and turned cartwheels until he was hot, dizzy and happy.

Suddenly, in the middle of the vast open space he felt he was being watched and came to his feet, turning slowly, trying to pierce the darkness. And then, though he failed to pierce the gloom with his eyes, he became aware of what seemed like a glow in the trees to his right. The moment the idea of a glow occurred to him he rejected it, for there was nothing to be seen. The glow remained even when he closed his eyes.

There was something there, somebody there. He knew this although he could hear nothing and see nothing, except in his mind. Almost at once he became aware that there were two people, a man and a woman, and they were not remotely interested in him, only in each other.

Still uneasy at the very idea of sex, he turned away, only to become aware of another glow, a different kind of glow. Under a bush (he had no idea how he knew it was under a bush, but he knew) lay a very unhappy creature, not conscious, not quite unconscious. He had been drinking but drink had failed him. He was cold, lonely, miserable. Somehow Bev knew there was nothing to be done for him. He was driven to be cold, lonely and miserable. It was his destiny, almost his wish.

Bev found all this fascinating but not surprising. In a park at night, still long before midnight, it was only to be expected, he supposed, that there would be half a dozen couples making love in the friendly dark, a few drunks, a derelict or two with nowhere to go, perhaps a few men with darker thoughts of theft and violence. It was not surprising to him that he could spot these people mentally, it was only surprising that he had not previously been able to do so.

Not one of them knew he was there. He could pick his way

softly through the park, passing within a few feet of the dozen or so people he now knew to be there, without his presence being suspected. Few of them cared anyway – only one dark glow far away at the extreme corner of the park represented danger, a sick personality whose very fears made him dangerous.

The wider implications of his discovery did not at the beginning occur to him. He thought only, with wonder, that he need not feel nervous of running into people unexpectedly, because he could spot the glows ahead and avoid them or hide.

One couple who were making love were getting no pleasure from it. They were almost as unhappy as the poor wreck under the bush. But for the most part the lovers radiated a wild delight which proved to him more than any words of Conan's that sex was something that no one who wished to be more alive could continue to ignore.

Cold now, nearly naked and inactive, he began to run again.

Only one girl had recently talked to him, the girl Conan had brought to see him. He knew her name, Sally Wells, and roughly where she lived – very roughly, for Bev scarcely knew the basic layout of the town in which he had spent twenty-four years. The very thought of the beautiful girl Sally Wells drew him and he thought *Why not*? He was out to taste freedom, to walk, to run, to glory in his new mobility, and the idea that he might possibly find Sally and savor her glow was attractive. He would not speak to her, merely find her if he could, and see if he could tell as he could tell of the people in the park whether she was happy or unhappy.

It was unlikely that he could find her. He was able to pinpoint the glows in the park because they were so few and so widely spaced in such a vast area. Out in the city again he would be swamped by the crowds of people in the houses lining the streets.

But that was all the more reason to try, to find out. He tried to see mentally beyond the park, and he was no more surprised to find he could not than he had been to find he could spot the presence of men and women in the darkness.

The fact that the park had many gates did not matter since they were all locked and he intended to climb out anyway. The derelict suburb where Conan had said Sally lived was in the south of the town, near the motorway, and Bev knew that his mother's house was on the north side of the park. That meant striking out in the opposite direction to his home, and this he found symbolically attractive.

He ran through the park, no longer as fast as he could go but in a gentle jog-trot which he found kept him warm without bringing him out in a sweat or making him breathless. It was easy to avoid the others in the park, but when he came to the railing that marked its southern extremity he found himself facing a brightly-lit street, in which there were quite a few pedestrians and even an occasional car.

It had been madness not to wear clothes, yet he did not regret coming out as he had done. He had always been warm, well wrapped up, submerged in blankets and woollen clothes and motherly devotion, and on the night he broke out it had been necessary, even obligatory, to do so virtually naked.

The snag was soon overcome. Few streets were well lit at night, and most of the lighting went out at midnight, which must be fast approaching. The next street, easily reached by picking his way along just inside the railing, being careful not to be seen by anyone outside the park, was unlit, silent, deserted, and it ran in the right direction.

The glow – he had rejected the word yet could not think of a better one – of human beings did in fact fade when there were too many of them. It seemed that if he could see a man or woman walking past less than fifty yards away the sight overrode any mental awareness. Perhaps the new vision worked only in the dark.

He climbed the fence and jog-trotted along the empty street. A vague memory that athletes and people trying to lose weight did this sort of thing, running about, often at night, often in light running clothes, came to him and eased his uneasy self-consciousness. There were not many athletes but there were some, he knew that. Boxing and football still drew crowds. Anyone who spotted him jogging along like that would stare for a second or two and then decide he was a boxer or footballer in training.

He was close to exhaustion, closer than he knew. Two weeks ago he had been used to being carried about. He had stood up only for a dozen times a day, walked no more than fifty yards and all within a house, seldom climbed stairs. He had achieved near miracles by the way he had driven himself since, but there had not been time to build up muscle and stamina.

Bev didn't know it, but he was a coward in small things and a hero in bigger things. He had been terrified of meeting anyone until he realized that if he did the stranger wouldn't even speak. Yet he made himself stagger on when what he needed was a hot drink and bed.

He got the hot drink, rather surprisingly. Reeling with exhaustion, he was warned by neither glow nor light and as he turned a corner found himself being stared at by an old man, a nightwatchman, with a hut and a brazier, in the middle of a deserted road.

'Lad, tha's reet puggled,' said the old man.

Beverley had never heard the accent of Yorkshire, and the words sounded like a foreign language to him. Yet he understood the old man's friendliness and there was something warmer and deeper in his glow than he had encountered before. He found himself smiling widely at the old man.

'Reet, lad, rest thysen,' said the watchman briskly, moving a foot along the wooden bench on which he was sitting. 'Nay, tha can't go another step. Tha's done too much already, to my way o' thinking. Here, have a mug o' tea and a bite of summat.'

Dazedly Bev sat down and accepted a steaming plastic mug. He was not fond of tea, but this was like no tea he had ever tasted – strong, dark, sweet and very hot. He discovered it was exactly what he wanted. And the thick sandwich that accompanied it – two hunks of bread with meat and pickle – was more enjoyable than any four-course meal he could remember.

The garrulous old man ran on without a pause, and presently Bev found that if he didn't concentrate too hard on the strange words and merely let the torrent flow over him, he could understand the sense well enough.

He had seen pictures of nightwatchmen with their braziers but never met one. Once the breed had become almost extinct, firms and factories relying on burglar alarms, electronic devices, stout locks and sprinkler systems to guard their property at night. But now the devices were becoming unreliable and it was easier and more effective to pay an old man to watch the premises. From where he sat the old Yorkshireman, whose name was Sam Clough, could watch the main entrances to five small factories. That was why his hut and brazier were set up in the middle of the road – he was more or less equidistant from the five factories, and there was little risk of traffic running into him, not at night.

The brazier, burning coke from one of the factories, threw out a great heat, which would have been necessary in midwinter but was too much on a summer evening, and even in his briefs Bev was soon awash with perspiration. The old man, wrapped up in shapeless jacket and trousers with colored muffler around his neck, didn't seem to notice the heat. Beverley suspected that in winter, sitting before the same brazier with snow all around, he wouldn't notice the cold either.

Gratifyingly he didn't seem to find it strange that Bev should be running around at night in trunks and plimsolls, and when Bev stood up to go on, wonderfully refreshed by the tea and food, and driven away by the fierce heat rather than by any desire to get away from the loquacious old man, Sam didn't try to detain him.

'Reet enough, lad, sit any longer and tha'll stiffen up. But don't do too much more. A hot bath and bed, that's what you need.'

Bev thought so too, but having come so far – he must now be fairly near Sally's house – he had no intention of giving up.

'I wish I could pay you for the food and drink,' he said, 'but – '

'Nay lad, none o' that or you and me will fall out.'

When Bev ran on, taking a minute or two to settle into his previous jog-trot, he was happier than he had ever been in his life. The old man had accepted him and Bev had had no difficulty in talking to him – largely, he had to admit, because nobody had to say much when Sam Clough was around. Perhaps that explained the old man's friendly hospitality – he merely wanted an audience.

Yet Bev knew on reflection it was more than that, and found himself comparing the company of the old man with that of his mother, the doctor, the housekeeper, the few other people he encountered regularly. He would much rather have Sam Clough.

He came to deserted houses and knew he was in the area where Sally lived, according to Conan. But the area was large. He looked for a glow and found none. There were people behind him, nobody in front. He might be standing at the edge of the world, unable to see it because of the darkness.

Then abruptly he knew he had to find Sally. By a weird coincidence he and someone else had come looking for her on the same night. He was not exactly aware of this, his awareness being vaguer. What he was aware of was rather that he had to reach Sally first.

Get Conan, he thought, and it was a good idea. Conan was a competent, experienced person, unlike himself. Besides, he knew Sally, Sally was his friend, and Bev hardly knew her at all. Conan would know what to do and be able to do it.

Unfortunately there was no way of getting Conan quickly. He had a phone and Bev knew the number, but the chances of finding a public phone in this area still working were negligible, and all the other places where he might find a phone were silent and dark and locked up. If anything was going to be done, he would have to do it himself.

He began to run again, though he still couldn't sense Sally. Why this should be he didn't know – was it possible that she had no glow? Far more likely was that she was somewhere else, perhaps staying with friends.

The other man, however, Bev could spot like the people in the park. And it was no wild guess that this other man was seeking Sally, and with no friendly intent. That was a certainty. Bev didn't even believe it was a coincidence that he was there, out on his own for the first time, on the very night that the girl was in danger. It seemed far more likely to him that he had unconsciously but correctly chosen that night.

It was a pity he had not unconsciously but correctly taken some sort of weapon with him. Not a gun – there was no gun at the house and Beverley would not have known how to use one if there were – but a knife, a stick, an iron bar. As it was he was not only unarmed, but very obviously unarmed . . .

Vince Hobley was unarmed too, for a very particular reason. To overpower Sally with the aid of a weapon would be a completely empty revenge.

He had waited perforce until the broken carpal bone on his right wrist was mended. The electrorestorer technique which Dr Anastasia Hersholt had so ofen used on Gardner repaired flesh and to some extent muscle, but it could do nothing for broken bones, and his right hand and wrist, though usable, still had to be treated with extreme care.

But Sally, in going for that wrist, had not known he was left-handed.

Vince was all in black and took great care not to be seen. For he was going to kill Sally, no less, and he was going to get away with it. Provided he was not seen, he was quite certain he would get away with it.

Since he had met Sally only once, in a lonely spot with no witnesses, it was scarcely possible that he could ever be traced. He had sprayed his fingertips with rubber solution and he had nothing on him by which he could be tracked down. The investigation, which would be inefficient and short-handed anyway, was doomed from the start.

A lot was going to happen before he killed Sally. As he crept nearer and nearer, he exulted over this in his mind.

This time he wouldn't make the mistake of giving her a chance. A clout on the side of the head, a heavy punch in the solar plexus, a jab in the belly and she would have lost the capacity to fight him off as she had done the first time. He would not harm her seriously, then, but he didn't mind the thought of her beauty being marred by bruises and dishevelled hair.

Then he would strip her and rape her. It would have to be rape – he shied away from the very idea of acquiescence or submission on her part. The initial brutal blows were necessary not only to break her resistance but to ensure that what happened subsequently would be rape.

After that . . . It had been sheer chance that in his fury the last time he had said: 'I'll break every bone in your body.' He had meant no more by it than people who used the threat generally meant. It was only later that he realized he could not only keep the promise, but keep it literally.

He was going to break every bone in her body.

At some time, inevitably, she would die. Arteries would be severed or internal injuries inflicted inadvertently, as he broke the larger and more important bones. But that would not be for a long time. He knew most of the bones in the body, where to find them and where to break them.

The bones of hands and arms first – then he would not have to bind her. Phalanges, metacarpals, carpals (like the bone of his she had broken), ulna, radius, humerus. Then the bones of feet and legs – and after that she would not be able to walk or run or stand up. Phalanges, metatarsals, tarsals, astragalus, tibia, fibula, patella, femur.

He would break them with a stone which he would take from her own garden. A round stone would do the job quite effectively. He had strength, and he was not particularly concerned about surgical accuracy.

Then – would she be unconscious? Would she have fainted? He would throw water over her naked, broken body if she did, before breaking it still more.

After that things would become tricky. Ribs next, and when he broke them, every one, floating ribs too, there would be a danger of puncturing her lungs or her heart and shortening the ordeal, which was not his intention. From then on he would have to improvise. Sternum, clavicle, scapula. Perhaps it would be an idea to fracture them before the ribs – easier and less dangerous.

Breaking the pelvic bones, the vertebrae and the skull would offer still more difficulty if she was not to die, and it was his plan that no single blow of his should kill her, but that she would die of pain. And then there were the teeth, the mandibles . . . probably, he had to admit, he would get nowhere near breaking every bone in her body before she died. People stoned to death in ancient times had died comparatively easily.

Despite the great pain potential of knocking out her teeth with a stone and breaking her jaw, he had already decided to reserve this for the unlikely contingency that he would succeed in doing all the rest and she would still be alive and at least partly conscious. Her face, her very pretty face, was to some extent her identity and he had no wish to torture a faceless thing. For that matter, he would avoid blood as much as possible . . .

Vince Hobley, a full Saxon if not a highly talented one, should certainly have known that there was someone on his trail, and no mere peasant at that. His Saxon awareness should have screamed it at him.

But Vince was wallowing in the filth of his imaginings. He would not have known if every Norman in Britain had been converging on him.

Bev was only a hundred yards behind when Hobley reached the house. Once again Bev probed, cautiously – the total absence of any glow but the black death of Vince almost convinced him that Hobley had gone to the wrong house or that it was empty, which would be the most satisfactory state of affairs. If Sally wasn't there, Hobley would be cheated and would have to go away, and Bev, quite thankfully now, could go home too.

But the grim certainty of the man in black did not diminish. He went round the house, followed cautiously by Bev, and selected a ground-floor window. He took something white and circular from his pocket, apparently licked it, and pressed it against the glass. Bev remembered the plastic suckers he had played with as a child. Then Vince took out something else – diamond or some other glass-cutter – and carefully cut the pane out of its frame, drew it out by the sucker and laid it on the ground. After that he looked around, and Bev froze behind a bush, thinking he had been spotted. But the man in black stooped and picked up a stone from a small rockery, turned back to the window and climbed inside.

Too late, Bev picked up another stone from the same rockery and realized he might have smashed it on the other man's head while he was concentrating on cutting the glass.

Bev crept cautiously to the window and listened. The man was already through this room and into the house beyond. Bev took off his shoes and left them under a bush, then climbed in carefully, making sure his skin was not torn by the cut glass. He took his stone with him.

Beyond this room, a sort of study (it had been David's), there was a faint light. At the top of the stairs was a skylight, and the light walls collected enough of the starlight for Bev, whose eyes had not been dazzled by any bright light for many minutes, to see quite clearly.

Vince, on the stairs, was stripping off all his clothes and

hanging them on the bannister. Even in the gloom Bev could see the dark hair not only on his chest and under his arms but also on his back, his legs, his belly. This, then, was a Saxon.

Vince stripped naked for many reasons – to ensure that there would be no blood on his clothes, for one – but mainly for the instinctive one, that he would come to Sally as an animal, a Saxon male. This time the situation was reversed – she was to know he was a Saxon, she was to feel thick fur against her smooth flesh.

Strangely, at the very last moment, when he had found a door behind which he could make out slow, even breathing, just before he threw it open, he had his first prickle of warning, a hint of another presence. But he suppressed it, brushed it aside, and crashed the door back on its hinges.

Sally woke at once, reached for the bedlight and switched it on.

Hobley, a jagged stone in his hand, was horrible. He was literally snarling, his face contorted at the unexpected onslaught of the light – he had meant to take the girl in the dark. The hair almost all over him made Sally's flesh creep, and to her there was something foul about his nakedness. She saw him tense to fling himself on her, and she threw back the bedclothes. Whatever chance she stood against him – and she recognized him and knew that once before she had conquered him – it was bound to be better if she was mobile on her feet rather than trapped by the sheets.

Her emergence made him pause. It would not be necessary to tear off her clothes. She slept nude. Also her total hairlessness made him hesitate. Could she be a Norman?

Sally leaped from the bed and grabbed a heavy metal hand-mirror. Now the stone he held was neutralized. If she could induce him to throw it, the result of this encounter might well be the same as the last.

Like Vince, she felt no need of words. His nakedness made his intention not merely obvious but undeniable, had he tried to deny it. Her eyes, however, were on nothing but the stone as she willed him to throw it, and as if obeying her he jerked his arm back.

'No,' said Bev in the doorway.

Vince whirled round. Sally, alert for any opportunity, had

a chance to smash the heavy mirror on his head. But she, like Vince, found herself frozen by the sight of the tall, pale figure in the doorway. Alone of the the three of them he was not nude, though he wore only dark briefs. Yet in a way it was as if he was naked and they were clad. He looked like a god, slim, white, sexless, serene. Sally noticed the stone he held in his hand , and it seemed right and proper that he should drop it casually, a mute but effective gesture, indicating that he had no need of it.

In fact, Bev dropped it when he realized that he could control the situation – he, who had never controlled anything in his life. He looked calmly at Vince, and Sally noticed, if he didn't, that the lust went out of Vince.

Bev exulted inwardly, knowing suddenly that Vince would not touch him. Bev had been prepared to fight, not knowing how, yet with a shrewd perception of the probability that he and the girl together might achieve something against the hairy Saxon. However, this was better. In every degree that the other man was lowered, he himself was raised.

Sally was less surprised at the moral collapse of Vince when she remembered that she had seen it before. Indeed, glad as she was that Bev had made this astonishing appearance (she had understood he was some kind of psychopathic would-be suicide even weaker physically than mentally), she thought she might have overcome Hobley without him, though probably at considerable cost.

At the moment when Sally and Bev independently decided Vince was beaten without a shot being fired, without a blow being struck, Vince threw himself at Bev.

Bev raised his hand. He didn't know what he intended to do. He certainly didn't mean to make a dramatic gesture of warning. But it stopped Vince, or rather changed the nature of his action. Instead of attacking Bev he became in a moment simply a man more than willing to leave, and Bev stepped aside and let him.

For the second time Vince Hobley, having approached Sally with lust, left with shame.

Bev, had Sally known it, was as deflated as Vince the moment he disappeared.

Sally was pink and nude and so disturbing to Bev that he could neither look at her nor look away. She waited, as he waited, for some audible indication that Vince had really gone. They heard him muttering on the stairs, evidently pulling on his clothes, and finally a door slammed. He could, of course, have slammed the door and waited inside to surprise them later, but Sally knew, as she had known once before, that when Vince was beaten he was beaten.

'Thank you,' said Sally quietly.

There could seldom have been a more embarrassed hero. Sally seemed to feel, having been nude all along in the company of both Vince and Bev, that there was no point in suddenly becoming modest. And indeed this was so. Though not exhibitionistic, Sally despised the flabby modesty of the peasants.

It was too late now to throw on a wrap. That would be coy, and Sally despised coyness too. She would no more put on clothes because people stared than she would take off clothes because they stared.

'Tell me all about it,' she said.

He found abruptly that he wanted to talk, particularly to this lovely girl. He wished she would put on some clothes, yet even that, as time passed, mattered less and less. The room was warm except for air currents from the open door, which presently Sally closed. She asked him if he wanted coffee and he refused, still replete with tea and food from the old nightwatchman.

She seemed to understand why he had worn only briefs and shoes as he climbed out into the night. He talked, he explained himself to himself as well as to her, and Sally gradually began to understand him and place him not just between the shining hero of a few minutes ago and the weak, frightened psychopath she had previously thought him to be, but somewhere else altogether.

And finally, quietly but firmly, she made him get into bed with her, not so much silencing his protests and doubts as not allowing him to make them or have them. Though he was older than she, there was something motherly in the way she took him to her, for she knew that he had to be wooed from cold motherliness to the warmth he had never got from his real mother.

But most of all she was just a girl giving because it was in her nature to give, because she was able to give, and only a little because in this case what she was giving assumed an unnatural, inflated, infinite value. It was because of the last fact that she *had* to make love to Bev, to set him free (after all, he had been prepared to give his life for her), but it was not because of this that she wanted to make love to him.

Gardner had meant to drive the two girls home, but he didn't have to. Dr Anastasia Hersholt had taken one hard look at them and another at him, and said she was taking them to hospital.

Gardner didn't particularly mind that, for he had a hold over the hospital. It needed certain things which only he could supply.

Thus he was still at the Chestnut Grove house when Vince phoned, and what Vince said was interesting. Waiting for Vince, Gardner amused himself by recalling every detail of that night's session.

The Seymour affair had proved far simpler than he expected. Frank Seymour was ready, almost eager, to put himself farther and deeper into Gardner's power – that was to be expected. Gardner knew his type. And then, when Gardner was ready, the invitation, the invitation Seymour felt he could not refuse, to what was really a very mild orgy as orgies went. However, Seymour saw unspeakable things, and he learned for the first time what Gardner was.

But by then he was committed, or he thought he was.

To build up pressure on the rest of the family was equally easy. Margaret Seymour soon found herself in massive debt, her avariciousness making her blind to the eventual cost of the things she found herself obtaining so easily.

Gardner was actually bored with the details of the conquest of the Seymour family – he had done such things so often that that part of the business, once successfully completed, was no longer of any interest to him. It was like betting on a sure thing. His great weapon was that unlike so many people in the sad, sick world of 2066 he took the world as he found it and made use of it. His financial empire, too, was beginning to bore him. It was not difficult to be the richest and most powerful man in Sherburn, and he was no longer greatly interested in being the richest and most powerful man in all England.

His obsession was more and more with the power to destroy, to terrify, to hurt.

Embroiling Frankie – that was simple. A girl he himself had bought and brutalized did it for him, lying, showing injuries inflicted by Gardner . . . really it was too elementary for a man who once had taken keen pleasure in schemes for breaking people who stood in his way.

No, what was exciting was what he could do to the Seymours now he had them. They were all conventional, all nervous, all scared of what people would say – even the apparently aggressive Margaret, who was strong only to her weak family. It was easy to ensure their silence.

And then . . .

That night he had had the girls Ethel, who was fourteen, and Gwen, thirteen. They had let him practise his form of sex on them through fear, and thereafter were still more bound to him through guilt. Neither had taken easily to the pleasures of pain. They didn't seem to understand. He didn't mind: there was pleasure to be gained through enthusiastic cooperation, but even more when there was none. He had enjoyed their terror more than their pain.

Uneasily, however, he was aware at the back of his pleasure that it was not infinite. After the Seymours, what? He would wring all the enjoyment there was to be wrung from them, all nine . . . but then?

He heard the front door open and a few seconds later Vince came in.

'Well?' said Gardner. 'How did it go?' It was only after he asked the question that he saw from Vince's expression it hadn't gone at all, and started to feel an interest he had not felt when he asked the question.

'Beat me,' said Vince.

'What?' Gardner could scarcely believe it.

Vince, proud of his strong, lean body, never risked it. He took pleasure in hurting, not in being hurt. Gardner had never managed to initiate him into the pleasures of the whip.

'I want the lash,' said Vince dully.

It would be a great pleasure to lash Vince into insensibility. Gardner realized more clearly than usual, in that moment, that the malice of the world was simply lack of interest and that those few who could keep going by keeping interest going, by continuing to care about something, were losing the battle to find something to care about. *After the Seymours, what?*

But here was interest. Almost as entertaining as lashing Vince would be finding out why he wanted the lash.

'Why?'

'You'll never find out from me.'

'That girl. It must be that girl. Sally. She beat you once before. Did she beat you again?'

'No. It was a man. A hairless man.'

Gardner nodded. He had had little to do with the Normans, and no Norman had ever been coerced willingly or unwillingly into this room.

But the Normans, at the moment, were nothing to him.

Vince shivered. 'He had power.'

'What kind of power?'

'How should I know? I couldn't touch him.'

'I could,' Gardner said thoughtfully. 'I'd like to touch him.' It could be another interest, another aim, another goal.

When you broke a human being, the quality of the experience depended very largely in how much you had achieved by doing so. The average peasant was not a great deal harder to break than an animal, and Gardner had tired of breaking animals long ago. Saxons were better, much better . . . Could it be that these Normans, who had never particularly interested him, would prove to be even more worth breaking?

'This girl – is she a Norman?'

'She could be. But I don't think so. Anyway, I don't want to talk. I want the lash.'

Vince wanted, needed pain. Unlike Gardner, he did not suffer silently. He screamed and moaned.

Gardner enjoyed the screams and moans. Between him and Vince Hobley there existed, or had existed, almost every possible relationship except one . . . this one. He had heard Vince moan in strange pleasures, but he had never before heard him scream.

He screwed the pleasure higher and higher. Earlier, with the little girls, he had been in control. It compounded the ecstasy now to let go. He lashed the bleeding body with vicious joy. The blood ran down the naked upper back to the fur below and matted it.

Then, suddenly, he stopped.

Strange.

Vince had not screamed for a long time. Now that he thought of it, now that some shreds of sanity returned, he realized that Vince had not even moaned for a long time.

He threw down the lash and approached the limp figure.

Vince wasn't unconscious. Vince was dead. He had been beaten to death.

Anastasia went straight round to Conan's flat on her return from the hospital and was relieved, though surprised, to find him at home and not yet in bed.

'I didn't get away till midnight,' he said. 'What can I do for you, Ana?'

'I'm worried about the Beast. I'm going to tell you who he is.'

'You don't have to break professional confidence. I know who he is. Arthur Gardner.'

'How do you know?'

He shrugged. She knew he was not an ordinary man, but he had never encouraged discussion of it and she had never pressed it.

'All right,' she said. 'How long have you known?'

'Since the day I went to see Beverley Daley.'

'How . . . oh, well.' She changed what she was going to ask and said instead: 'How's he doing?'

'Incredibly,' Conan said briefly, and suddenly knew that the word, as far as Anastasia was concerned, had become literally exact.

It was rare for a Norman to have visions. Saxons had them sometimes. Or they claimed to have. Yet he knew that Bev and Sally were together, and he felt a pang . . . Sally he had nearly loved, or thought he loved, or wished he could truly love, and now she and Bev were closer than he and she would ever be. It was far more than the mere fact that Bev and Sally were lovers – he would have promoted that if he could on the day he took Sally to see Bev, if it was going to release a Norman. Bev and

Sally were something more . . . it was a case where two and two added up to at least five.

There was, however, a certain relief in the knowledge, a worry removed.

That other unusual, brief foreknowledge – that he and Sally would never be lovers – had bothered him. At the time it seemed to mean that either he or Sally had to die. Now it meant nothing of the sort. It merely meant that Sally's destiny was to meet somebody else . . .

Thoughts of Sally and Bev faded as what Anastasia was saying forced itself on his consciousness.

She had been called that evening to treat two young girls, thirteen and fourteen, after Gardner had finished with them.

Terrified, more terrified than hurt – though they were hurt badly enough – they had been as closemouthed as Gardner's adult victims invariably were. She had gathered, nevertheless, that they were only two of a family of nine completely in Gardner's power.

'We have to do something about this, Conan,' she said. 'There's never been anything like this before.'

'Yes,' said Conan. The Normans didn't interfere with the Saxons, or vice versa. They were not so much in uneasy alliance against the peasants as grimly aware that they could not afford to rock the boat yet. But there were certain unwritten laws. Gardner was rocking the boat.

There was a reason for the existence of Normans and Saxons, a purpose. Both believed they were the race of the future. Each feared secretly that the other might be the one to survive. Yet both knew that their purpose in the broad sweep of the history of the human race might be simply as an irritant, something to force the peasants to shake off their apathy and fight for existence.

'Yes,' Conan said again. Megalomania could affect both Normans and Saxons. He himself had once had to act God and let a certain Norman die.

It was not murder. In a great fire at a hotel in the city he had had the opportunity to save a few lives. To some extent he had control of the lives he saved and therefore, conversely, of the lives that were not saved. He could have let ten peasants die and saved John Dundee, one of the oldest known true

Normans. But Dundee had recently been trying to organize the Normans with a view to taking over the city – with himself as overlord, of course.

Conan had saved the ten peasants.

'I'll see about it,' he said.

Anastasia looked at him doubtfully. 'What will you do?'

'I don't know,' he said honestly. There was one thing, however, he intended to do first.

See Meredith Dundee.

He saw him early the next morning.

Meredith Dundee was a huge man in his fifties, and he lived in one of the few luxury homes which remained luxury homes. Conan found him climbing from his heated outdoor swimming-pool, the early morning sun gleaming on the golden hair that covered his body.

Comparatively old as he was, Meredith was one of the few Saxons Conan was forced to consider a magnificent animal. The hair on his body did not seem disgusting as Saxon hair generally did to most Normans. Perhaps because it was sleek, short, golden, it made him a magnificent animal rather than a degraded human.

Meredith took the towel a servant offered him, waved the servant away, and looked at Conan steadily as he towelled himself briskly.

'There's got to be a point in this visit, Conan Hersholt,' he said. 'Let's skip the preliminaries.'

'No,' said Conan. 'One or two preliminaries are important. John Dundee was your cousin, wasn't he?'

Meredith sat down on a plastic-covered divan and motioned Conan to sit opposite him. 'Yes,' he said. 'You know that.'

'No, I was never quite sure. I knew there was some relationship. I always wondered.'

'So did I. You killed John and you never bothered me till now. Why?'

'I didn't kill John. You were full cousins?'

'We had the same grandparents. His father and my father were brothers. You don't get cousins fuller than that.'

Meredith remained hostile, watchful. He let the towel drop on the ground.

Conan unzipped his tunic and dropped it on the ground too. They faced each other grimly, Norman and Saxon, naked.

'Meredith,' said Conan, 'if the Saxons here in Sherburn have a leader it's you and if the Normans have a leader it's me.'

'And if you hadn't killed John, it would have been him.'

'I didn't kill John Dundee.'

'You didn't save him.'

'At the cost of ten peasants? No. Perhaps you'll admit something and then we can make progress. Admit that you thought I'd have done anything in my power to save John, and that you were surprised I didn't.'

Meredith nodded grudgingly.

'That's enough in the way of preliminaries. You know Arthur Gardner?'

'I've heard of him. Naturally.'

'Never met him?'

'Not to my knowledge.'

'You know he's a Saxon?'

Meredith shrugged. 'No, but a man like that has to be something. He couldn't be a peasant.'

'He's becoming dangerous. To all of us.'

Meredith's gaze became even more hostile. 'So he has to be got rid of. A Saxon. Destroyed by Norman-Saxon agreement. That's worthy of you, Conan Hersholt.'

Conan stood up. He stooped, picked up his tunic, and zipped it on. 'Meredith, you've got power. Use it. Find out about Arthur Gardner. Maybe after that you'll come and see me.'

He turned and took three steps. Then as something occurred to him he turned back and said: 'John had a sister who married a farmer, didn't he?'

'No,' Meredith replied, cautious, suspicious. '*I* had a sister who married a farmer. Ian Callendar. Why?'

'Haven't you seen your niece lately?'

'Jan? What about her?'

'Find out,' said Conan, and went round the side of the house.

Meredith thought for a moment, then went into the house, locked himself in the windowless library and opened the safe. He took out a small notebook. The book was blank except for three pages of names. Some were in red, some in black. Some, like *John Dundee*, in red, were scored out. Some red names were scored out in red, some in black. The name *John Dundee* was scored out in red. The last name, *Arleen Jones,* was in black and scored out in black.

He wrote *Arthur Gardner* in black and then wondered why he should take Conan's word for it. He had never taken anybody's word over any name he had entered in that book. Yet on reflection he nodded, satisfied that Conan wouldn't think him fool enough to take anything he said on trust. Conan had said *Find out about Arthur Gardner,* knowing he would. Therefore Gardner was a Saxon.

Jan Callendar? Little Jan? He saw her seldom because he and his sister had never got on. Blood was seldom thicker than water between Saxon-peasant siblings.

But if Jan was a Saxon – or a Norman – he would certainly take a greater interest in her. Suppose he invited her to stay with him for a while? Meredith did not think her father would refuse. A canny husbandman, he would not wish to sever any link which might eventually in any way prove profitable.

Meredith, a careful man himself, never meddled in the Norman-Saxon-peasant situation except to cool it. He owned the Sherburn newspaper not to disseminate the truth but to suppress it. He was not even curious. His little notebook could have been much fuller if he had spent money finding out about Normans and Saxons instead of merely noting names when chance brought a revelation.

But a niece, pretty little Jan . . . Saxon or Norman, she must be given her chance, whatever she wanted to make of it, and whether she wanted to make anything of it or not.

The servant returned. 'Telephone call,' he said, and before Meredith protested, as he invariably did, hating to be disturbed, added: 'I believe it's fairly important, sir. Otherwise I wouldn't have – '

'Who is it?'

'Arthur Gardner.'

The coincidence did not surprise Meredith, who was used to coincidence. He lived with coincidence. All Saxons and Normans did. Their extra awareness made coincidence happen. It was natural that at the moment Gardner became important to him, Gardner should elect to call him on the phone.

Gardner said: 'Dundee, you don't know me but you know

about me. Perhaps you don't know I'm a Saxon, but I am.'

'I haven't the slightest idea what you're talking about.'

'No? Then you soon will. Dundee, I'm in trouble. I've killed a man. A Saxon. It was an accident, but in the circumstances nobody will see it my way. I can square most things, but maybe not murder.'

'I can see there might be some difficulty.'

'Anyway, I'm not going to try. I've decided the best form of defence is attack. I'm going to organize the Saxons, bring them out in the open.'

Meredith dropped the pretence of ignorance. 'No,' he said sharply. 'Don't do that.'

'What's the alternative? Can you get me off the murder charge?'

'No. There's still law –'

'I know that, and that's why I'm going to get Saxons around me. Form a group, a force, an army. To take over . . . I don't want to fight you. I want you with me.'

'That can't be. Gardner, don't you understand that there are Saxons and Normans all over Britain, all over the world, and they've tacitly decided against coming into the open and against making any such challenge? We all know that we must not –'

'Think it over,' Gardner interrupted. 'Then get in touch with me.' And the phone went dead.

After Bev left her, Sally slept healthily. And she had a dream . . .

On the whole it was a happy dream, happier than any since her early childhood, though it was not all happy. And when she came to herself in the morning she did so drowsily, with unusual reluctance, tried to recapture the dream, and when she failed, tried to remember it.

At some kind of party – the details were vague – she met somebody. Of course it was Bev, though he too was vague, sensed rather than clearly seen. He didn't make much impression at first, although it was obvious that he was very attractive. She pondered long over that – in the dream she knew and acknowledged his good looks from the first moment, yet was not herself attracted to him.

Strangely, too, Conan, who was also present, was quite clear.

And she talked with Conan, not Bev. Without her noticing, Bev quietly moved elsewhere, and she saw him several times with other people, other groups, who were as indistinct as he was.

It was only when she suddenly became aware that he had left that she missed him. Then she really missed him. It seemed incredible that she should have made no effort to keep him with her.

Time passed – hours or days. She had to go somewhere. She was going away. And at the last moment she knew she had to see Bev again. She didn't know exactly where he lived, though she felt sure she could find him if she tried.

Then, with the abruptness of dreams, he and she were together again. Now there was no doubt that they were in love. The nagging though not painful sense of loss was gone.

And that was all the dream. There was no more.

Sally had fancied herself in love before. She had never, however, felt wonder and relief that she was loved in return. Neither shy nor particularly modest, she took it for granted that if she wanted any man, there would be no particular difficulty in getting him.

This time what she sensed all the way through the dream, even from the beginning when Conan loomed in her thoughts, was the warmth of Bev towards her, a warmth she simply could not turn away from. Once they were together, there was no question of parting again. She wouldn't be such a fool twice . . .

Thinking about it with her eyes still closed, she wondered if it meant anything. The dream was not erotic. She and Bev kissed, they stood passively and contentedly in each other's arms, but they were happy to be together without passion.

And this was all very surprising, since when she went to sleep it was after an extremely passionate episode with Bev and no particular thought of love in her mind.

One thing did mean something. She felt now exactly as she had done early in the dream, when she had let Bev go and berated herself as a fool for doing so. Perhaps the dream was not a recapitulation but a prophecy.

Did she love Bev? Of course she loved Bev. And that day she would find him. From what she had heard Mrs Daley could be no problem. The thought of being afraid of her naturally didn't cross Sally's mind; the only danger was that Bev still couldn't break away from her, and that didn't seem much of a danger.

From things he had let drop, Sally knew that Bev generally slept late and that in the afternoons Mrs Daley was usually with her cats. The obvious thing to do was to tidy up all the business of the day before lunch and then go and see Bev.

She was neither nervous nor doubtful about the outcome. Whether the dream meant anything or not, Sally knew what she wanted and she was used to getting what she wanted.

4

Arthur Gardner was late going to the factory that morning. Before he made his move he wanted every employee to be there and he wanted work going in full swing.

Two minutes after his arrival the place was in turmoil.

The managers, the executives, the top office staff told him he couldn't close the factory, just like that. It was not possible. So he started at the bottom and worked up, personally firing everybody. The office boys, the juniors, the typists and clerks didn't put up a fight. They left apathetically. And the men on the top rungs of the ladder found the rungs below them demolished.

He sent for the foremen and told them to stop production. They didn't argue either. There could be a hundred reasons for the stoppage, and to simplify matters and avoid argument he spoke not of dismissal or permanent closure but rather of a temporary suspension of production. After all, some day he would probably want to open the factory again. Even if he didn't, he expected to be begged on all sides to do so, and he might need a good bargaining position.

But not everybody was sent home. From every department certain men and women were sent to the boardroom – clerk Harry Chubb, typists Glenda Morris and Joan Bush, engineers Tom Barton, Jim Simon and John Breaks, production line girls Harriet Price, Angela Devine, Diana MacLeod, Helen Sims . . .

Seymour he simply fired. He enjoyed that. Seymour, for all his fear and shame and horror over what was happening to his family, had gone on believing that this was part of the price for the top job in design he was going to get. He had clung to this desperately, refusing to doubt, wildly hoping that when he eventually got it a miracle would happen and with the new responsibility he would somehow acquire power over his own destiny and the nightmare would be over.

Now Gardner casually told him: 'I'll have to let you go, Frank.' Gardner was not a master of words. Not for him the subtle tortures which some men could inflict on others merely by talking. However, he remembered good phrases and he had always felt, 'I'll have to let you go,' was a far more satisfying way of dismissing a man than telling him bluntly: 'You're fired.'

'But our deal . . . ' Seymour faltered.

'What deal?' Gardner asked unblinkingly. 'Oh, you mean the arrangements I made with certain members of your family? That'll have to stop too, I'm afraid. I'm going to be too busy from now on. Pity.'

Seymour forced himself to persist. 'You promised me a top job in design – '

'Oh, that. Yes, I did, Frank. I did.' He paused to enjoy Seymour's relief that he was not going to deny this. 'But naturally you could only get a top job in design if there was work going on here. And I'm closing the factory, so the job you want doesn't exist.'

Seymour turned away dully.

As an afterthought Gardner said: 'If you've got money problems, Frank, well there I can help you. Your youngest girl, Meg, hasn't visited me yet. Busy as I'm going to be, I'm sure I could find time for her. Eight, isn't she? And very pretty in the picture you showed me.'

Seymour stood transfixed. A moment ago he had thought everything between Gardner and himself and his family was severed. Now he wished this was so.

'I haven't paid much before,' Gardner mused. 'I haven't felt it necessary. You were in my power, Frank. Your whole family was in my power. Paying you more would have put you less, not more, under my control. Now things are different. For Meg . . . say two hundred pounds? No, I'll be generous. Two hundred and fifty.'

From the look on Seymour's face he knew he had him. Not now, when the family was not badly off. But in a few weeks when their situation was really desperate, the knowledge that they could have two hundred and fifty pounds merely for something that would happen to Meg, something they wouldn't have to watch, something that probably would not leave her permanently damaged physically, would work on them until they convinced themselves that they really had no choice.

It flashed into his mind suddenly, brilliantly, that he might not have to return Meg alive. He could allow himself to torture her to death. After all, the Seymours were in his power. And if he got away with killing Vince, why not others? If his plans worked...

He had taken Vince's body in the car and dumped it in a lake, wrapped in iron chains. The efficient, resourceful police of a century ago would probably have found it, but the chances were overwhelmingly against it being found now. That was no worry. All he had to fear was that the continued absence of Vince Hobley would be noticed – after all, the pair of them had been inseparables – and questions would be asked.

If all went well, if he succeeded in transforming the situation, his life and the town, no one would ask questions. He would speak with anger of Vince who had walked out on him at the time when he needed him most.

It was a pity he had admitted so much to Meredith Dundee. But he had really believed Dundee would join him . . . he still might. Sooner or later Saxons had to unite against the Normans and peasants. That was obvious. Anyway, Dundee would never actively go against him, Saxon against Saxon. Arthur Gardner, who trusted nothing and nobody, was completely certain of that.

'Still here, Frank?' he said. 'I thought you'd gone. Remember – Meg. I want her.' In a burst of perverted generosity, knowing he was going to kill Meg and not merely return her damaged but alive, as Seymour believed, he said: 'I'll make it five hundred. Five hundred, Frank. But that's all. No more.'

After this interlude with Seymour things moved more and more quickly. Gardner did not own every stick and stone of Sherburn Plastics, and if a real leader had emerged to coordinate opposition he might have been defeated in his plan to halt the factory in an hour.

But no leader did emerge, and before eleven o'clock Gardner

was alone in the vast factory except for the seventy or eighty men and women who had been sent to wait in the boardroom.

He went to the boardroom.

Bev did sleep late, his door locked as was usual now, and woke up finally at eleven o'clock with mixed feelings both physical and mental.

Sally had wanted him to stay with her, but he had left at four, convinced Hobley would not return. He had walked and run home, and was so exhausted when he arrived that he was quite incapable of getting in again the way he got out. Fortunately he had learned how to get into the house without a key and the room next to his was empty. The two windows were together, indeed, part of the same frame, and he was able – just able – to drag himself into his own room and climb into bed, still in his trunks.

He wakened stiff and sore but not tired. On the contrary, he wanted to go out and chop down a tree or climb a mountain. Since neither was practicable, he made his way cautiously and unseen to the bathroom and had a hot shower. Then, with spartan determination, he had a cold shower, emerging tingling, feeling good, and more desirous still of cutting down a tree.

Abruptly it came to him that more than cutting down a tree, more than having a sumptuous breakfast, what he really wanted was Sally. And he could have had her if he had stayed with her . . . or could he?

Bev, emerging from the shadows, becoming a man, beginning to become more than a man, remained in some ways reserved and modest. That Sally should be prepared to give herself to her rescuer seemed entirely natural and did her no disservice in his eyes. Quite the reverse. It seemed almost inevitable.

But this was a new day. Sally was a wonderful girl, and he was nothing in particular. If he wanted Sally, he would have to win her. Their hour of passion the night before was finished. If they began again, it would have to be on a new footing.

Like many another man before him, he wanted sex and had to settle for something else.

Having crept about the house making sure he was not seen

by his mother or Sarah, he found to his relief, annoyance and amusement that he was alone in the house anyway. After the first relief annoyance dominated – he wanted something to eat, and besides, it hardly seemed possible that after such a night his doting mother and the conscientious Sarah should simply have gone out leaving him alone in the house.

It was only after his brief irritation burned itself out that he remembered his mother and Sarah knew nothing of the momentous happenings of the last few hours. They thought he had slept as usual, stayed in his room as usual, and was as indifferent to food and drink as usual. His mother would be with her cats and Sarah, probably, shopping.

In dressing-gown and slippers he entered the kitchen for the first time in years and looked around him. There was nobody in Sherburn, perhaps nobody in England, who knew less about preparing food than Bev Daley. He did not even know how to operate a gas cooker.

He was hungry enough, however, not to care if his food was hot or cold. He found bread, tomatoes, cold meat, eggs. The contents of bottles and jars soon revealed themselves to him. He made sandwiches and drank a glass of milk.

His only failure in his first attempt to forage for himself was with the eggs. He knew eggs had to be cooked and when he encountered warm eggs in their shells they invariably proved to be soft-boiled. Cold eggs in their shells were always hard-boiled. Without thinking he assumed that the cold eggs in the refrigerator were hard-boiled, and stared in dismay and disgust when he cracked one and found it raw.

No eggs, then.

He was surprised but not displeased to find that even when he thought himself ravenous, eating more than he needed did not appeal to him. A couple of tomato sandwiches, two cold meat sandwiches with sauce and pickle, and he was satisfied.

Exercise was now a necessity. He wanted to do as he had done the night before, put on briefs and shoes and go for a trot through the park. However, he now knew that this would attract attention he wanted to avoid. He found shorts and soft-soled shoes, put them on, and was looking for a suitable sweater when the doorbell rang.

The glow was of a friend. He didn't hesitate. He went to

the door, thinking happily it must be Sally, forgetting that Sally had no glow.

It was a disappointment when he opened the door and found it was Conan.

'Well, well,' said Conan, entering and closing the door behind him. 'Quite a change.'

'Yes. I'm going out for a run in the park. Want to come?'

'By all means,' said Conan mildly. 'How long has this been going on?'

'Only since last night, I went to see Sally Wells – '

'I know.'

Bev grasped his arm eagerly. 'You know? You can sense things? Know them, without knowing how or why?'

'I gather you've discovered you can? After you and Sally . . . found each other?'

'No, before.'

'Before? That's interesting.'

'Tell me, Conan, what are we? Who are we?'

'Something special,' said Conan soberly. 'Perhaps freaks. They're special.'

'There must be a purpose.'

'Of course there's a purpose. When you find out what it is, let me know.'

'You don't know?'

'I can guess. Anybody can guess. Your guess may be better than mine. In fact, I'm beginning to suspect it will be.'

'Sally,' said Bev regretfully, 'has no glow.'

'Glow?'

'That's what I called it.'

'Elan, no. Aura, yes. Only maybe you don't know how to look for it.'

'Elan? Aura?'

'The words are not important – they're convenient labels. What you and I feel – this – that's elan. What we call elan. It proves you're a Norman and I'm a Norman. There's a certain rather different sort of . . . glow, if you like, that enables us to identify Saxons – sometimes. Peasants you can't sense – '

'I can.'

'Yes, so I gather. You may have something more than the rest of us. But to come back to aura . . . that's something more like the atmosphere people have around them, and Sally not only has it, she's got more of it than anybody else I ever knew. I can't tell you where to look or how to look, but don't worry about it. The next time you see her, you're bound to begin to see it. It builds up – '

'She's definitely no Norman?'

'Definitely.'

'But she's wonderful.'

'I know what you mean. I can sense her aura. I'm sorry, too, that she's not a Norman.'

'Conan, I don't know much about this. But I think there's some mistake about the peasants all being . . . peasants. Not only Sally. Last night I met a fine old man, Sam Clough – '

'An old man,' said Conan gently, 'could have been born before all this started. Before Normans and Saxons, and before peasants were peasants.'

'Yes, that's so. But Sally?'

'I don't know. How about that run in the park?'

There were chairs for only about twenty people in the board-room. Fifty or more stood about, murmuring, wondering.

When Gardner came in he went to the head of the table, and a space was cleared for him. The muttering intensified for a moment and then died as he held up his hand.

Glenda Morris was standing, as he had asked her to, against the dark curtains at the end of the room, just behind him. He caught her eye and she nodded. He had not told her much – a word or two, no more, a request, with no reasons given. She had been inclined to refuse or at least to argue.

But now she nodded.

She had been a willing partner in some of his secret sessions – for kicks and for money. After a time, however, she told him the money wasn't all that important and she preferred to get her kicks elsewhere and in other ways. But she went on working in the factory, calmly, efficiently.

She was a tall blonde, slim but wide-hipped. Without being pretty she was extremely attractive. Whenever she moved people looked at her legs. She wore a short blue button-through dress and no stockings. She looked, to those who knew about such things, like a proud and defiant Norman.

'Glenda,' he said. Just one word, but it was enough to bring comprehension to the faces of some of the people around him. Two girls, Angela Devine and one he didn't know, turned to the door to leave.

'No,' he said sharply. 'Nobody leaves. Nobody. Barton, lock the door.'

'Don't do it,' somebody said. It was John Breaks. He was a short swarthy man, one of the few who could be detected as a Saxon whatever he wore. And his eyes made it clear he was speaking to both Gardner and Glenda.

They both ignored him. Glenda made a slight bow in acknowledgment of the fact that every eye was upon her, and to ensure that every eye stayed on her. She slowly undid the buttons of her dress, one at a time, but kept it close about her. Then unhurriedly she slipped it off her shoulders and let it drop to the floor.

The reaction was delayed, a double-take. For a moment everybody – or at least everybody to whom what was happening was coming as a surprise – thought she was clad in a golden swimsuit. A moment later there were gasps, exclamations, even a stifled scream as they realized that she was naked and the soft golden coat which covered her torso was her own. Unlike most Saxons, she was furred over the navel and over the breasts. The golden coat stopped abruptly almost exactly where a one-piece swimsuit would have done at groin and bust, leaving legs, arms and shoulders bare and browner than the golden coat. Closer inspection suggested that she was carefully depilated so that she could wear short dresses, even a one-piece swimsuit, without revealing a square inch of fur.

Gardner's gaze turned on Breaks and moved on. He didn't want a refusal, and Breaks would refuse.

Anyway, he couldn't stand apart from this. He had to declare himself. For effect he would have liked a splendid male Saxon specimen, like Vince Hobley, a fitting complement to the magnificent Glenda, to expose himself. But there was effect, too, in giving the example himself.

He threw off his clothes willy-nilly. Unlike Glenda he had not taken time to prepare himself so that the revelation could be immediate. On the other hand, those ignorant enough to be surprised were progressively shocked, interested, puzzled or repelled as they saw his black-haired upper body, only a little more furry than that of many ordinary men, then the plump legs, looking as if they were clad in black furry long johns, and finally the thickly-coated belly with only the operative part of the massive reproduction organs hairless.

It had to go on. No pause could be allowed. The orgy of revelation and declaration had to gain momentum, not lose it. 'Barton!' Gardner called to the man at the door, half-way down the long room. 'Take off your clothes.'

Mechanically Barton took off his overalls and the shirt he wore underneath. Every eye turned from the cool Glenda and the squat Gardner to the tall, thin and flustered Barton. He didn't take off his shorts, shaking his head emphatically. Nevertheless, the dark fur all over him suggested he was no less furry than Gardner, probably more so.

But Gardner wasn't satisfied. 'I said take off your clothes,' he said sharply. And Barton, who for a Saxon had not much more resistance to pressure than a peasant, obeyed.

Beside Gardner, Glenda bent to pick up her dress, evidently thinking the show was over. 'Don't touch it,' said Gardner. 'You'll never wear it again. We don't need clothes, we Saxons. We all know that, don't we? Wearing clothes has been our shame. Let's cast out shame. Diana, Harriet, Joan!'

Two of the three girls did not move. The third, Joan Bush, began with a strange defiance to take off her blouse, slowly and deliberately. Gardner eyed her narrowly. She and Glenda were colleagues, thought to be very close friends. There were the usual rumors of lesbianism, rumors which Gardner knew to be false, for Glenda was decidedly heterosexual.

Removal of Joan's blouse revealed no hair like Glenda's. Removal of the bra likewise. She stepped out of her short skirt and a tall fair-haired man, Lionel Davoe, said: 'No, Joan. Let's get out of here.' He tried to take Joan's hand, but she pushed his arm away.

Now with challenge in her manner and open defiance she stripped herself nude and stood as straight and proud as Glenda.

She was totally hairless, in complete contrast to Glenda. And Gardner knew there was no disguise about it. She was a Norman, and knew it, and knew what it meant.

In seconds the scene became chaos. Some tried to get out. Some moved away from the two nude girls. Some moved towards them. And many men and women threw off their clothes, while others tried to tear off the clothes of those next to them. Furry bodies emerged, hairless bodies – but not another as hairless as Joan Bush. Lionel Davoe took no part except to push back people who tried to get too close to her.

Gardner's guesses proved good. Many furry bodies were revealed, those of fourteen men and fifteen women.

'Saxons, all of you,' he shouted. 'Come up this end.' And segregation started.

Many of those present, Saxon, Norman or peasant, remained bewildered. It was being demonstrated undeniably that there were three kinds of people, but what this meant they didn't know. Some, like Glenda Morris, John Breaks and Angela Devine, knew they were Saxons and always had known . . . the last two refused to take part in the orgy of stripping, but they moved slowly to the Saxons' end of the room.

Only Joan revealed herself as a Norman. Many others, unable to prove themselves Saxon or Norman, took off their clothes anyway, but generally not them all, and thus proved nothing at all.

Deliberately Joan Bush and the man with her moved to the other end of the room, past the confused group who were neither Norman nor Saxon.

Gardner had tried to pick all who could be Saxon. He had made no special effort to include all who might be Normans; he guessed that for many reasons there were few Normans working in his factory.

Joan Bush was a surprise. He had thought her a probable peasant, a possible Saxon. Besides, she should have known what was in the wind and had had the chance to refuse to go to the boardroom. Some others had. Some of those must be Normans.

It was clear, however, that the defiance she had shown and was still showing was the keynote of Joan's presence. She had attended the meeting deliberately, knowing what it was all about, willing to expose herself as a Norman.

A black-haired Saxon, furry as an ape, suddenly decided to take his own action about Joan Bush. He jumped on the long table, the only free space in the crowded room, and ran down it, straight at Joan.

Joan simply looked at him. Careering down the table, his bridges burned, he found himself wishing he had stayed with his friends at the other end. But he had to go through with it.

Instead of launching himself on Joan from the table, smashing her to the floor, he found himself stepping gingerly off it. She was less than three feet from him. The man with her stood back, his arms folded.

The ape found that he could not do a thing. His lust died – a thing which had never happened to him before. He told himself the hairless woman was ugly, unattractive. Yet five seconds before he had not found her so.

He wanted to strike her down, as if that was what he had intended all along, but couldn't even do that. He turned and pushed his way back to the head of the table, handling the peasants roughly to restore his ego.

Joan didn't press her luck. She might hold off a crazed Saxon who had just found out he was a Saxon, but if the rest of them wanted to humiliate her, beat her, rape her or kill her – a strong possibility – there was no way to stop them. She pulled on her clothes again and moved up the room to the locked door. Lionel went with her.

Then, as Lionel stayed at the door, she walked into Saxon territory, looking at no one but Glenda Morris.

'I'm going, Glenda,' she said. 'What about you?'

Glenda shrugged her shoulders, smiled slightly and gestured at those around her. The message couldn't have been clearer in words. *I'm a Saxon. You're a Norman. I have to stay. You have to go.*

Gardner, throughout, did nothing and said nothing. He exulted when the ape went for Joan, hoping for blood, sex, victory for the Saxon, defeat for the Norman. When the ape failed Gardner wanted to call on his Saxons, his new army, to fall on the defiant Norman and kill her. But this new army was scarcely formed yet. They might not obey. Indeed, he guessed from a quick movement by Glenda when Joan seemed about to be overcome – the only quick movement she had made during the entire incident – that Glenda would not stand for anything happening to Joan.

So when Joan turned to Barton, holding out her hand for the key, Gardner said: 'Let them out. Her and the man. Nobody else.'

The forty peasants surged to the door when it was opened. They wanted to go too. About half of them, caught in the excitement of the mass stripping, had taken off their clothes. Some of these were naked. Now that it was clear, however, that for them there was no point in the gesture, that they had neither lost nor won, that they were not in the game at all, they were all furtively putting their clothes back on.

'Wait!' Gardner snapped, and, used to obeying him, they stopped long enough for Barton to get the door closed and locked after the departing man and girl. 'We've got to get this settled once and for all. Any one of you who feels he belongs with us, let him step forward. This hair business isn't definitive. Glenda, you tell them.'

She didn't mind: she liked the limelight. No one else had made an impression to match hers, even Joan. Absence of hair proved very little. She was proud of her golden-coated body and looked forward to allowing the fur to grow on her legs, shoulders, back and arms.

'Nobody else is like me,' she said. 'Even the men, see, have bare patches. But you may be a true Saxon all the same. Some of you standing there among the peasants are true Saxons. Declare yourselves. We've skulked in the shadows long enough – '

'No!' John Breaks exclaimed. Although he had joined the group at the end of the room, he had not taken off a single garment. 'Listen, all of you. This is something we can't take back. All over the world Saxons are lying low – and they're right. The time will come, but it hasn't come yet – '

'I say it has!' Gardner shouted. 'From now on no Saxon conceals himself. If he does, we disown him. We have fur like the animals. From now on we go about like the animals. What do you say?'

He had not asked them until he was sure of the answer. There was a shout of approval, and the Saxons who had not stripped to the fur began to do so.

Even Breaks, after long hesitation, shrugged and revealed

a black coat more complete than Glenda's, for his arms and legs and shoulders were covered too.

'We march!' Gardner said. 'The Saxons march!'

There were shouts of 'Where?' and 'Against what?'

'Against the world. Where? To our new headquarters.'

He looked once more at the peasants. All he said was: 'For the last time . . . '

Three more people, a girl and two men, revealed themselves as Saxons and joined the group. To the others Gardner said: 'Right, now you can go. You can't help being peasants. But tell the others. Tell everybody.'

Sally visited both shops by cycle as usual, and then returned to the house in Chestnut Drive. With David and Arleen gone, she thought, she'd have to devote closer attention to the shops. She could use the flat above the Cornwall Place shop, the one below Arleen's.

She went back to the house to pick up the books and correspondence she kept there, and some clothes.

After a brisk run in the park with Bev, who stayed there, Conan had to go to the fire station. He was going out on a call when Meredith Dundee arrived at the station, driving his gray Rolls-Royce.

'Where's the fire?' he demanded.

'At a rubbish dump.'

'Forget it. Something's happened, more important than any fire. You've got a new job.'

Conan smiled. 'That's the second new job I've been offered. I didn't take the other one either.'

'You'll take this one. Gardner's going to blow everything.'

'Can't you stop him? Why do you need me?'

'Because I'm not organized any more than you Normans are.'

'You're proposing a Norman-Saxon alliance?'

'For this. Norman-Saxon-peasant. Get Jan Callendar. And your sister. I know about a dozen Saxons who'll be with me, not Gardner – '

'How did you find out about Jan Callendar?'

'Guessed. What about the Normans, Hersholt? Where will they stand?'

'Let's get this straight. You and I, and anyone we can persuade to join in, are going to fight the Saxons?'

'Don't be a fool, Hersholt. I'm a Saxon. The last thing I want is a Saxon-Norman war, or a Saxon-peasant war. But Gardner is organizing the Saxons and he's blowing all cover. He killed a man, did I tell you? A Saxon. So we can get police backing – '

'To do what?' Conan insisted.

'For Christ's sake use your head, Hersholt. How do I know? I don't know what Gardner's doing. But I can keep things out of the Sherburn paper if necessary, and maybe we can isolate the town. If we move as fast as Gardner, or faster, at least we'll have something to take action with . . . How many Normans are there?'

Conan didn't get a chance to answer, for Joan Bush and Lionel Davoe hurried up, looking for him, and stopped dead at sight of Meredith Dundee.

'If you've got something to say,' Conan said, 'go ahead. Meredith and I have an understanding.'

Meredith looked at him quizzically. 'I'm glad to hear it. I was beginning to wonder.'

Joan, the events of the boardroom still fresh in her mind, stared at Meredith with considerable distrust, but Lionel said quietly: 'It's all right, Joan. His aura's okay. I get the feeling he's with us against Gardner.'

'Marvellous,' said Meredith tartly. 'That's what I've just been saying.'

'What you *say* doesn't particularly matter,' Lionel retorted. 'What I *know* is something else entirely. I'll tell you both what happened.' And he poured out the story of the scene at the factory, supplemented, after some hesitation, by Joan.

'More than thirty Saxons,' said Meredith. 'That's quite a force. I don't know if I can count on as many.'

Conan made up his mind. 'Joan, Lionel. Get in touch with all the Normans you know. Tell them – '

'Tell them to go straight to my house,' said Meredith. 'Listen, you two. I don't want Saxons destroyed. I don't want anybody destroyed. I want things to return to what they were twenty-four hours ago. So do you. Maybe it can never happen. But so long as that's what we all want, we can work together. Perhaps, too, once Gardner's Saxons know I'm on the other side, some of them will leave him for me.'

Conan nodded. He had already thought of this.

The ordinary Saxon and the ordinary Norman – if any member of either race could be called ordinary – had an inbuilt leaning toward hiding in the crowd. This arose not from fear but from caution. *In the country of the blind, the one-eyed man is killed.*

Also, since both races consisted of individuals, there was no natural move toward forming a group. If there were new instincts, they were not gregarious instincts.

The peasants were incurious, and it could be taken for granted that at the head of all the communication outlets were Normans or Saxons. And they all knew that for every Norman or Saxon there must be at least twenty children who would develop one day . . .

It was so obviously reasonable to wait.

But Gardner was blowing everything. Something had to be done. And wasn't a Saxon-Norman alliance a wonderful thing?

Even more wonderful if it became a Norman-Saxon-peasant alliance and the human race came together again.

Joan and Lionel departed on foot, Conan left the van at the station and they set out in Meredith's Rolls.

'There's one Norman we can pick up on the way,' Conan said. 'Bev Daley.'

Bev was still in the park, trotting doggedly round the perimeter. He wore only shorts and shoes, having left his tracksuit under a tree.

As he ran off to retrieve it, Meredith mused: 'I wonder if Gardner's right in one thing, that we're meant to throw off our clothes. A century ago nudity was becoming more and more commonplace, but in the last fifty years the trend has been very much the other way. Then along came the Saxons . . . we don't really need clothes, you know, anyway only in dead of winter. You're different, of course –'

'Not so different. Our skin looks tender, but it's actually tougher, thicker and more elastic. We have a high resistance to cold. There's also a subcutaneous layer –'

'Really?' Meredith was interested. 'That must have been for a purpose.'

'Maybe just greater survival value.'

'And maybe you as well as us have been made independent of clothes. It's not just physical. Only perverted Saxons – and I admit more Saxons go wrong than Normans – have a feeling of shame about their bodies. Of course they hide themselves, as that girl Glenda did until today. But they're very willing to stop doing so, as she proved.'

'The point, if there is one,' Conan mused, 'may be wider than you think. Sally Wells is the most remarkable peasant I ever met. And most of the time she wears shorts and not much else.'

'Who's Sally Wells? Oh – the girl who owns the food stores. I thought she was a Norman.'

'No.'

'Really? Well, you should know.'

Bev came running back, breathless. He was carrying his tracksuit but had not put it on.

'I tried a cast around,' he gasped. 'I know where Gardner and the Saxons went. They marched out of the factory and they've gone straight to a row of houses Gardner owns on the outskirts of town.'

Meredith looked at him thoughtfully. 'Not many Normans can do that. It seems you really have some special gift.'

'And Sally,' Bev went on, ignoring him, 'is alone in her house in the next street!'

At the head of thirty naked Saxons Gardner marched through the streets to the row of houses he had bought for privacy. He had never intended to use them for anything like this.

People in the streets stared and then timidly turned away, not knowing what they feared, but afraid.

Gardner shouted: 'Join us . . . if you can!' Two men and two women did join them; there were thirty-eight naked Saxons when they reached their destination.

Glenda, who had elected herself second-in-command, surveyed the shabby street with no great enthusiasm. She said, however: 'I suppose it will do. We have to stay together, and we've got this whole area to ourselves. We do have it to ourselves?' she asked Gardner.

It was only then that he remembered Sally. He knew now that David was dead and she lived alone. Dark schemes began to form in his mind.

He knew his little Saxon army would not yet stand for anything extreme. He had not told them he was already a killer, and only a few of them, like Glenda and John Breaks, knew of his private passions. Glenda had been here before but had been brought and taken away in a closed van. She was seeing the place in daylight for the first time.

It was his destiny to be at the head of a reign of terror, but he was shrewdly aware that his followers had to be led into committing themselves gradually. Had the feeling of the meeting earlier been to tear Joan Bush to pieces, he would have led them joyfully. But it had been quite clear that they were not ready for any such thing.

If Sally was at her house and he knew she generally lunched there – this was a chance to begin to mold his group.

'There's a girl,' he said. 'A peasant. She'll have to go.' He looked around. 'Chubb, Barton, Simon, Thomson – go and bring her here.' He pointed. 'You'll know the house. It's the only one occupied.'

That was the way to do it, he exulted. If the entire thirty-eight went, it might turn out to be another incident like that of Joan Bush. The moderates, particularly Glenda, would agree that the girl should be told to go, but unharmed. The four men he sent would not return without the girl – they would lose too much face before the others. Sally wouldn't come willingly. They'd have to handle her roughly.

They might even kill her. And though he didn't want her killed, that might serve his purpose too. He'd have four murderers and thirty-four accessories to murder.

He took the others first to the house with the torture chamber, but did not show them the torture chamber. That would come later, when his control over them was total. There he unlocked a drawer and distributed house keys, twenty-seven of them. Those who wanted a house to themselves could have it, meantime. However, they were already splitting up into twos and threes or small groups.

Glenda stayed behind with him when the others had gone to inspect their new property. 'Just what are you planning, long-term?' she asked.

Gardner said carefully: 'I'd be a fool to plan anything long-term just yet. We'll have to play it by ear. Bringing in more people is the first move. We'll combine that with getting supplies and weapons.'

'Weapons?' Her tone was sharp, disapproving. Quite unlike her usual cool tone. 'Why do we need weapons?'

'We have to be able to defend ourselves. Suppose they send the whole police force against us?'

'Charging us with what?'

'Breaking the peace. Indecent exposure. They could easily think of something. Long-term, Glenda – we rule. We take power. We become the masters.'

She nodded. She went along with that. Good. This was how it would be done. Foot by foot she would go along with him, like the rest . . . until it was too late to go back.

There were shouts outside, and they went out to see what was happening.

The four men were back – with Sally. And the thirty-odd Saxons were lined along the road, on both sides, jeering and shouting crude insults.

Sally had not come willingly. Her blouse was torn, predictably, and there was a bruise on her cheek. Her hair hung over one eye and occasionally she licked a cut lip.

She was not cowed and she was saying nothing, saving her breath for fighting. It took all four of them to drag her along.

There was no telling how a crowd would react. The Saxons along the seedy road might have cried 'Shame!' and run to help her. But her beauty brought out lust in the men and jealousy in the women. And she was obviously not one of them. They wanted to see her beaten, humiliated, broken.

Gardner literally rubbed his hands. This was exactly what was needed. He was quite prepared to give up his own plans for Sally and surrender her if there was any chance that the Saxons would commit themselves over her, vent their inborn hatred of non-Saxons in a way that could not be quietly forgiven and forgotten afterwards.

And then Glenda, once more, stepped in. 'Stop that,' she

said sharply. 'We don't even know the girl. At least I don't. She'll have to go – this is our territory. But that's all. Let her go.'

The four men looked at Gardner, and the jeering stopped.

He nodded reluctantly. The moment had come and gone. If Glenda hadn't intervened, somebody would have thrown a stone, a girl would have stepped forward and spat in Sally's face, and when she went down they would have kicked and stamped on her. But Glenda, without tongue-lashing them, without rousing their ire, had restored normality.

The four men let Sally go. She took one step away from them and looked wonderingly at the naked Saxons. She learned a lot from that one glance. Sometimes words were not necessary.

Then she walked, straight and determined, to Gardner and Glenda.

'Thanks,' she said to Glenda. 'You and I could get along, Goldie.'

'We're not going to try,' said Glenda coolly.

'No? I've a strong feeling you don't belong with this lot.'

'You're wrong. I do.'

'Break it up,' said Gardner shortly. 'You. Get out of here.'

'I'm not You, I'm Sally Wells. And you're Arthur Gardner. Where's your friend, the one I threw in the river? I don't see him here.'

Glenda shot a quick glance at Gardner. Until then she had assumed Vince Hobley had some other job to do, like rounding up Saxons.

Gardner felt her gaze on him and had to commit himself. Later he could have said Hobley was a false Saxon who stood in the way and had to be removed. Or if chance gave him the opportunity, he could have said the Normans killed him.

Now he had to stick to the first story. He put anger in his voice and said: 'He walked out on me when I needed him most. But why am I telling this to you? You've got a chance to get out of here with a whole skin. Take it.'

'No,' said Sally. 'Not yet.' Sometimes she really was foolhardy. 'I'm a peasant, so the Normans won't tell me anything. Except one Norman who doesn't know anything. What about the Saxons? What will you tell me?'

There was no argument; Bev wouldn't argue. He said he was going after Sally alone, and he went.

Nobody had to tell him about his newly-awakened awareness. When he sought certain answers, they were there. Others were not. There were limits to what he could do, and he was gradually learning the limits empirically.

He knew as he ran once more, in daylight this time, towards Sally's house, that the Saxons had found her. He knew when she was being hurt and he knew that her head was bloody but unbowed. There was a moment when he knew she was safe, and he groaned aloud when a few seconds later she was once again in danger. Although the details were not available to him, he was aware that it was Sally's own courage, obstinacy and curiosity that put her in danger again.

The Saxons had some rudimentary form of precognition. It was evidently very unreliable, otherwise no Saxon would ever do the wrong thing. It seemed to work very much as isolated moments of precognition had always worked, most clearly and strongly when what was revealed didn't particularly matter.

In this Bev was right. Vince had not known the night before that his plans concerning Sally were going to fail miserably, that Bev would be there, that later when he sought pain and self-abasement it was going to end in his death. Gardner had not known he was killing Vince; in a sense it was not murder because there was no intent to kill.

Few of the Saxons sent to the boardroom at the factory had known why they were there and what was going to come of it. Yet Glenda, given a hint, had seen most of what followed long before it happened.

Arleen Jones had known *before* David died that he was going to die. She knew where although not precisely how. But she had not known when that day dawned that it was going to be her last on earth.

Bev was already aware that as a Norman he had no such ability. He had never known what was going to happen and he suspected he never would. What he knew was certain human *feelings*, his own and those of others. That agreed with what Conan had told him about empathy.

He knew now he loved Sally, and with that love lay fear.

With Sally he could be a strong man, more than a strong man, a Norman. Without her he would be Beverley Daley again, the poor ghost of a human being who, finding life not particularly worth living, had decided unconsciously to end it by not drinking enough to sustain life.

Now he knew how Arleen Jones had felt. If he lost Sally, he lost everything. He would return to his mother, his new awareness would fall from him, he would never run again, he would let the Normans and Saxons get on with it because for him it didn't matter any more.

'So you want to know,' Gardner said softly. 'All right, come inside.'

'You little fool,' said Glenda dispassionately. 'You've already had a taste of what he'll do to you, and you want more?'

'I want to know,' said Sally obstinately, 'what he intends, what you all intend. Then maybe I'll go. When I'm ready. Not before.'

The Saxons who had lined the street and jeered at her were turning away, opening the doors of the house and going inside. Gardner, Sally and Glenda still stood outside the house of torture.

'Come inside,' said Gardner again.

Glenda said directly to Sally: 'Listen, I'm not coming in with you. I saved you once, and I'm not going to do it again. If you go in with him, you're on your own.'

Sally walked boldly into the house.

She knew she was acting unreasonably. There was more of obstinacy than anything else in her attitude.

Yet there was a certain shrewd calculation behind it too. When she left she would go to Bev and Conan, and they would want to know what had happened and what she had seen. She was mulishly determined not to go until she had learned something.

As much as anything else, what set her apart from the peasant was curiosity. She *wanted* to go into Gardner's house.

Besides, she remained practical. The physical threat of the short, tubby Gardner she treated with contempt. She had handled Vince Hobley, and beside him Gardner was nothing.

Naked he obviously had no weapons, and she intended to make sure he didn't get a chance to lay his hands on any.

Glenda's refusal to come in with them did not bother Sally. Glenda, after all, was a Saxon, big and strong and a doubtful ally. She might side with Gardner. Sally preferred to have nobody but Gardner to handle.

Gardner took her downstairs to the torture chamber. For a moment Sally looked around her uncomprehendingly. She had not grown up in a world of TV spectaculars, historical films, magazine fiction. She had not seen films of the stories of Edgar Allan Poe, or melodramas in which beautiful maidens were stretched on the rack. She looked at the rack and could not figure out what it was for. The Iron Maiden was like a grotesque suit of armor, the pincers like the tools of a blacksmith, the thumbscrews merely curious antiques.

But the purpose of the whipping posts was obvious. And she realized that the stains on the floor were dried blood.

'This,' said Gardner happily, 'used to be my hobby. It used to be secret. I used to have to pay my victims. Not any more. Now this room and the things in it are going to help me to rule.'

'Rule what?'

'You name it. First my own people. Some of them know the pleasures of pain already. A small demonstration, very little really, will ensure solidarity such as hasn't been seen this century. Then we'll turn outwards. Peasants will be brought here. Old men and women, pretty girls like you. You know how Hitler worked? No, I should have known. You've never even heard of Hitler. He enslaved a people, nearly the world. He did it by fear and pain and dogma.'

His hand went out to pick up a whip. Sally snatched it from him and threw it in a far corner of the room.

Gardner didn't seem to mind. 'We've already got the dogma,' he said. 'The Saxons will throw off the Normans and take over England. Every Saxon will come to us, because we'll spread the Nazi net of fear. Those not with us are against us. The scapegoats, the victims, will not be the Jews this time but the peasants. To prove they're not peasants, the Saxons will have to prove they're Saxons. To prove they're Saxons they have to line up with us here.'

The frightening thing, Sally thought, was that it could work.

'You think everybody's just going to let this happen?' she asked.

'Yes,' he said confidently. 'You know the peasants will – '

'Except me.'

'True. But you, my dear, are one in a million. All the other peasants will do as they're told, as they always do. I made a fortune just by manipulating peasants. Now I'm going to do much more.'

'Rule the world?' she said sarcastically.

'Why not? All that's needed is ruthlessness and patience. I've got both. First Sherburn. How long would you say it'll take? Three weeks? A month? Then other towns. Not London until London's encircled, so that there's no place for the peasant millions to go.'

Sally would normally have been impatient with this sort of stuff. Even the fact that it was all possible, which she had already acknowledged to herself, would not have induced her to go on listening. But when a madman, a dangerous madman, was prepared to talk, she was prepared to listen. Next time he might not be so willing to talk.

Gardner showed one sudden flash of Norman awareness. 'You wonder why I tell you this, before I'm really ready? For one thing, there's nothing you can do to stop me. For another, you're not going anywhere. Ever. You had your chance and you wouldn't take it.'

He came at her. Sally hit him, coldly and deliberately, on the navel. He gasped and staggered back. She followed, hitting him on the mouth.

He was even less of an obstacle in her path than she had expected. It occurred to her that if she killed him, which she could quite easily do, a lot of trouble would be saved. She didn't believe that Glenda or any of the other Saxons would go ahead with anything remotely resembling Gardner's plans.

But she couldn't kill him. She had no moral scruples but several practical ones. Law and order had to be not merely restored but strengthened, and as a deliberate killer, even of Gardner, she would have to submit herself to the law.

Gardner was on the floor, by the wall, heaving, green. She took her eyes off him for a moment, measuring the distance to the door.

She underestimated him. She underestimated him because she did not take into account the fact that he enjoyed pain, took pleasure in being beaten. Where another man would have stayed down, helpless, afraid of further punishment, he rolled suddenly to a small cupboard set low in the wall and came up with a long knife in his hand.

Sally watched the knife narrowly. It wasn't a gun, which would have turned the tables unequivocally. She still had a chance. She would make him take a wild swing at her and miss, and if she once caught his pudgy wrist she would throw him, knife and all, and with luck she would kill him in honest self-defense.

But he didn't make a wild swing. He came at her slowly, determined not to lose the advantage this time, content not to kill but to disable, cutting her hands, her arms, her legs.

And then he had a vision.

It was absolutely clear. He was on the floor of the torture chamber, face down, naked, the long knife in his back. And Sally bent over him, unharmed, pulled out the knife and looked down at him with calm satisfaction.

He had had one or two such warnings before, like all Saxons. Usually a vision told him something unimportant or only moderately important. But he had known that a gas tank was going to explode and had just enough time to take cover before the blast killed twenty of his workers.

What he saw wasn't necessarily inevitable. It showed what would happen *if*. If he went for Sally with the knife, she would get it from him somehow and he would be dead.

He gestured with the knife. 'Get out,' he said, and this time Sally didn't argue. She was out of the house in seven seconds.

Only then did Gardner realize something that might have made a big difference.

The vision still clear in his mind, he saw that Sally wasn't dressed right. She was not wearing the torn blouse and blue skirt, but a red bra and red shorts.

That meant the vision could apply to another occasion. Perhaps, with a chance to kill her and the vision, he had let her go for the vision to come true.

No.

He still, he thought with a certain relief that he had not made a stupid mistake, had had to let her go.

Visions, dreams, warnings did not explain themselves. Sally could have got the knife from him, killed him and left him where he lay, the knife still in his back – and later, having brought her friends, having changed her clothes, she could have triumphantly shown them what had happened, pulling out the knife and looking down on him.

What he must ensure was that Sally was killed but not by him; that the knife he still held in his hand was destroyed; that Sally was never in his presence again.

There was another way: burn the house, blow up the torture chamber, leave the street, so that he could never be found in this room with a knife in his back.

That, however, was further than he was prepared to go. He was going to need the torture chamber. Premonitions were not absolute. Quite possibly he had dissolved this one by not allowing the girl to fight him for the knife, by letting her go.

He went to the front door. Glenda, fortunately, was not in sight. He sent for Chubb, Barton, Simon, Thomson – the same four.

'That girl,' he said. 'Sally Wells. She's escaped. With vital information. Go after her and kill her.'

They stared at him. They were not ready for this.

'You're protected. You're with us. You're Saxons, and she's an enemy. Get her, kill her. Any way you like. But make sure.'

It was an important moment. He had already started building up power over his small band of specialists. Every moment it was more difficult for any of them to turn back.

But if they flatly refused, if they stood together and said there was to be no killing, he would be back to square one. He knew he did not possess the personal magnetism of a born leader. He could not command by personality. He had to command by fear.

'Well?' he said. 'What are you waiting for?'

'Kill her?' said Barton.

'She knows too much.'

Surprisingly, the old cliché worked. Barton nodded, Simon nodded.

Gardner nearly said: 'Bring back her head.' He wanted to say it – later he would say such things and expect to be obeyed. But it was too soon.

5

Normans and Saxons were on the move. Both groups had certain supernormal awarenesses; both were proud of them and feared them; neither had ever fully used them.

All over the world for half a century Saxons had been born, one in many thousands. In some countries they came early, in some they came late. Underdeveloped countries had few Saxon births – it was the nations farther along the road, with more complex if not bigger problems, that had more Saxons sooner. And nobody knew about it, for Saxons did not become Saxons until puberty or later. When they did finally develop, the first thing was the most obvious, their hairiness. And nearly all, being alone, were shocked and horrified to find themselves different, like none of their friends. They shaved themselves, hid their bodies.

All over the world for half a century Normans had been born, one in many thousands. Like the Saxons, they didn't develop until the age of sixteen at least, sometimes as late as twenty-five, sometimes never. But their problems were less. True, many male Normans were ashamed when they found they did not develop hirsute proof of their virility. However, this as a rule was of very little moment, for their voices deepened and their virility was clearly greater than that of most normal adolescents.

Only in England, naturally, were they Normans and Saxons. In America the Normans were still Newmen, the Saxons Sexers. In France the Saxons called themselves simply *les hommes* and *les femmes*. The Normans were *les nouveaux*. In Spain both groups called themselves *fértil*, and disputed each other's right to the title. In Germany both gave themselves long portmanteau-word titles which became abbreviated to *Simco* for Saxons and *Eleben* for Normans.

Without agreement, without discussion, without national or international congresses, everybody stayed under cover more or less. If there had still been nationwide television, even nationwide radio, curious news gatherers would have unearthed and disseminated certain facts that in the end must have exposed the situation. But there was no longer any such organization. A man might discover the curious fact that his brother was totally hairless, a woman might discover the even more curious fact that her sister was covered with fine hair like some small furry animal . . . these discoveries were not advertised.

Yet at the same time there was no ironclad secrecy. Conan Hersholt had kept no record, but in fact he had had sex with five hundred and seventeen girls, of whom five hundred were peasants, fifteen Normans, and two Saxons. All of these knew he was no ordinary man (virility alone was not ordinary), and two or three hundred, either at the time or later, had had a hint of the truth, that he was a Norman (whether or not they knew Normans by that name).

The existence of three types of human beings, three distinct types with distinct characteristics, was uneasily known, uneasily suppressed. Normans, perhaps the most stable of the three races, knew intuitively that drawing attention to their existence could not be a good thing. Saxons, the least stable, had a morbid fear of imprisonment, and stepping out of line could mean imprisonment. The peasants just didn't want to know.

'The really interesting problem,' Meredith mused to Conan after Bev had left them, 'is why and how this present situation came about. There's never been a confrontation in London as far as I know, or Bristol, or Birmingham . . . why in Sherburn? Is this the flashpoint that will set the whole world on fire? Or is it simply a minor local disturbance of a type that's happened a hundred thousand times before and has always been extinguished by some natural force that we don't know anything about through lack of communication?'

The four Saxons sent after Sally to kill her might have done it. They would probably have had to work up to it, pulling her about again until in retaliation she hurt them and they got angry and battered her to death in anger, half in frustrated lust.

Anyway they missed her for the simple reason that Sally, instead of running for her life as fast as her legs would carry her, in a straight line away from Gardner and the other Saxons, calmly returned to her own house to replace her torn blouse and pick up the things she had just packed. From there her route to the center of town was parallel to, but did not coincide with the way taken by her pursuers, who were far ahead of her.

Bev found her, however. She dropped her bags and they ran into each other's arms.

Sally was surprised and interested to find that she wanted Bev to make love to her there and then, in the deserted run-down street in which they met. She didn't give in to the impulse, not considering it sensible or practical. But she could not resist asking Bev if he felt the same.

Bev was slightly shocked. 'I want to marry you, Sally,' he said. 'I want us to be married when we make love again.'

'So we're on the way to the altar? How about one for the road?'

But he was in no mood for levity. Sally sobered too, as they exchanged news and walked on.

Their absorption in each other, however, was too great to allow even a crisis to divert them for long. And Sally found herself telling Bev about her dream.

She expected some interest, but was not prepared for his rapt attention. He stopped walking, put down the case he had taken from her and stared at her.

'I know it's strange,' she said, 'but not as strange as all that?'

'Sally, don't you understand? That was my dream, not yours.'

He went on talking, explaining it to himself as well as to her. Yet from the first moment she really needed no explanation, the pieces falling into place now she had the clue.

'When I first met you, Conan was there – '

'The *first* time! I never thought about the first time. I thought the meeting in the dream was when you appeared in the doorway and Vince Hobley ran away.'

'No, it was the first time. Naturally I didn't make much

impression on you. But you made a big impression on me. You were beautiful, you were friendly . . . What puzzled you was that there was no attraction. I wasn't attracted to you, I was frightened. But then when you'd gone . . . That was when I missed you. Your words were exactly true – it seemed incredible that I should have made no effort to keep you by my side. Days passed. I made myself stronger. I had to see you again – '

'Was it all reversed?' she murmured. 'The warmth . . . '

'That was my perception of *your* warmth. Let's be honest about it, Sally. The dream didn't mean that you love me. It meant that I love you.'

'Yet we had it at the same time. Of course, that's why Conan was clear and you were vague. Doesn't it mean anything that we had the same dream at the same time?'

'Only that I'm a Norman,' he said soberly, 'whatever that is. Somehow I was able to impose my dream on you.'

Sally, having decided not to be convinced, didn't argue. In her, the least sentimental of women, there was nevertheless a certain sentimentality. That she and Bev could even share a dream confirmed to her their rightness for each other.

When Bev and Sally arrived at Meredith Dundee's house there was no surprise, no glad cry of relief . . . for they knew already.

There were fourteen Normans and seven Saxons there, whispering, arguing, eyeing each other uneasily – but together.

The gifts of both Normans and Saxons were unreliable, erratic, even sometimes wholly lacking at the moment of greatest need. But a dozen Normans plus half a dozen Saxons could not all go blank at once. Something which a Saxon sensed was taken up by others, sharpened, modified. The Normans' quite different perceptions, focused on the same object, added color to a monochrome picture.

Meredith was the one who talked most, putting what the others sensed into words. The Normans didn't have to talk much. Jan Callendar stood with Conan, and there was no anxiety in them, for they were together.

Sally told them there had been nearly forty Saxons when she left, with more coming in. 'And there's only twenty-two of us here.'

'Twenty-three,' said Dr Anastasia Hersholt, coming round the side of the house. She wore a smart white suit, in startling contrast to the motley collection round the pool. Nobody was quite naked, like Gardner's Saxons, but nearly everybody felt compelled to show he or she was not a peasant . . . Even Sally, with bare legs and wearing a short skirt, proclaimed that if she was a peasant she was no ordinary one.

Ignoring the strangeness of the circumstances and the scene, Anastasia said: 'What on earth is the idea of the three gates at the side of the house, all unlocked but with those maddening springs and latches?'

Meredith Dundee stepped forward to welcome her. 'Simple, doctor,' he said. 'They keep out no Norman or Saxon and they didn't keep out Sally Wells or you. But they keep out everybody else – everybody who is liable to lose interest and give up.'

As he and Conan briefly explained the situation to Anastasia, as far as they knew it, three Saxons arrived, two men and a girl – all naked. They had nearly joined Gardner, then thought of Meredith Dundee and went to see which way he was going to jump.

A little later there was a surprise for Bev. Sam Clough, the nightwatchman, appeared, and after looking all around him, slowly took off his ancient jacket and threadbare shirt to reveal an old, pale, rather flabby body so completely hairless that they knew – after looking closely at his weatherbeaten but abnormally smooth chin – that here was the oldest Norman in Sherburn.

Bev moved over to him, pulling Sally with him, and the old man beamed at them and started to talk – not, of course, about the current situation or why he was there, but about anything and everything else.

So it went on. It was becoming very hot, and it was hard to remember that there might soon be fighting and that some of the people present might die.

Meredith caught Conan's eye, and Conan nodded. They had to be reminded, these fifteen Normans, ten Saxons and two peasants, that they were not gathered together to sunbathe round a swimming pool.

'We have to fight,' Meredith said.

'Of course,' Sally agreed.

They all fell silent. The Normans were uneasy – the Normans were not fighters. The Saxons were doubtful – they had joined Meredith Dundee rather than the extremist Gardner, but they were not entirely happy about opposing their own kind and allying themselves with Normans.

'We have to fight,' Meredith insisted, 'because of what Gardner is going to do. I scarcely know him and some of you know him well. Yet I think I know better than any of you what has happened and what he's going to do . . . because to read Gardner I only have to look within myself.'

Anastasia did not take her eyes off his face. Secretly she had always been drawn to men who were hairy and virile. She had tried to suppress the feeling, believing it to be neurotic. Now she was not so sure. She knew that Meredith's cousin had been a Norman, and that Jan Callendar was Meredith's niece. More, apparently, than anyone else, she found the implication staggering. She knew, too, from Conan, that Sally, one remarkable non-Norman-non-Saxon, had a natural aversion for Saxons . . . while she, another uncommon non-Norman-non-Saxon, with a Norman brother, felt no attraction toward Norman men and was greatly attracted by Meredith . . .

'Saxons love power,' Meredith said. 'Gardner and I are the two most powerful men in Sherburn. Five years ago, ten years ago, we were the two most powerful men in Sherburn. And I've been tempted to do what Gardner is doing now – '

'And why didn't you?' Sally demanded.

'It needs ruthlessness,' said Meredith bluntly, 'a quality I don't lack. It also needs cruelty, a quality I hope I do lack. No, I'll be honest. I could be cruel, but I've always tried to control it.'

'Surely,' Conan said, 'Gardner must have done something of the same sort, since otherwise he would have done long ago what he's doing only now?'

'No.' Joan Bush took a hand. 'I've known about Arthur Gardner for a long time. I've watched him. If I hadn't had a certain moral weakness, I'd have killed him.'

'You worked for him, hating him?' Sally asked curiously.

'Not quite that. My feeling never got personal. He never harmed me directly. If he had, I might have been able to act.

What I want to say is, he never controlled his cruelty. He's always given it full reign. I think why what happened today has never happened before is because there's a deep fear in him.'

Meredith nodded. 'You're right. Not until he killed a man – and ironically, I believe it's true that he had no intention of killing him – did he feel himself forced to come out in the open – '

'And you say you know what he'll do,' said Sally the practical. 'Exactly what is he going to do?'

Meredith told them.

The agreement that in the interests of all of them, Normans, Saxons and peasants, Gardner had to be stopped before he had a chance to get properly started was unanimous.

The Battle of Sherburn took place the next day . . . Thursday, August 5, 2066.

Meredith, having won his main point, lost his second - that the twenty-seven of them should march straight out into London Road immediately, armed or unarmed, and publicly seek a confrontation with Gardner and his Saxons. Conan pointed out that more people were coming in and that a further effort at recruitment might in a few hours tip the scales in their favor.

He was wrong – the next day there were twenty Normans, fifteen Saxons and still just two peasants gathered at Meredith's house . . . but Gardner had more than sixty Saxons and an auxiliary force. His organization was not better than Meredith's, but it was more single-minded. When Conan's people contacted a Norman, he had a choice. When Gardner's people contacted an uncommitted Saxon, he had no choice . . . not after a young Saxon who refused was skewered through the abdomen to a wooden stretcher and carried around by a van on the Saxon recruiting drive – dying but obviously not dead. There were no more refusals.

Gardner's Saxons were committed now.

London Road had been planned as the showpiece of Sherburn. It was broad and lined with trees. All the big stores and office buildings were there. Now the big stores were partitioned up or empty, and only a tenth of the office accommodation was used for its original purpose. But the street was still straight and spacious, and there were remnants of its past glory.

Knowing Gardner's Saxons were already marching from the south, the Norman-Saxon allies gathered outside Meredith's house. Every Norman and every Saxon was naked. Anastasia was in her immaculate white suit, proving nothing in particular except that she was Anastasia, and Sally, who thought going into battle naked or even half naked a silly idea, wore a white shirt and blue jeans, refusing to pretend to be a Norman or demonstrate that she was no Saxon.

There had been some argument, the main counter-proposal being that since Gardner's group were naked they should be different. But Meredith pointed out that the most important thing about their group was that they were Saxons, Normans and peasants, while Gardner's followers were all Saxons – and that should be clear to all.

This proved to be only technically true. Bev, whose perceptions and analyses of aura were quicker and surer than those of any of the others, said before there was any sign of the other group: 'They're sending a force of peasants first. About a hundred of them.'

'I don't like the sound of that,' said Sally.

'Neither does anybody else,' Meredith said grimly. 'Gardner wants us to fight peasants, maybe kill a few of them. Whatever we say or do later, that's not going to make the rest of the peasants love us.'

'We can't kill peasants,' said Conan firmly.

'So we surrender?'

'Normans don't kill.'

'I think I could have killed Vince Hobley,' Bev said, 'if it had been necessary.'

'That's different. I can't kill peasants even if they kill me.'

'Saxons can,' said Meredith, looking around, and there was a murmur from the other Saxons. 'Does that mean you Normans are opting out?'

'No,' said Bev mildly. 'Killing may not be necessary.'

The peasants were in view now, and with no word of command the Norman-Saxon troop started walking towards them. Deliberately they broke step and formed no ranks. Gardner's Saxons had marched in ranks, and everything this group did had to be different.

The peasants were clothed and armed with sticks. As the distance lessened, it could be seen that they kept glancing uneasily behind them.

'Unwilling warriors,' said Conan with satisfaction.

'Your head can still be split by an unwilling swipe with a stick,' Sally observed. 'And I just caught a glimpse of some of the Saxons behind them. They've got guns.'

'You don't have to worry about guns,' said Conan confidently. Some of the others were not so sure.

'Wait,' Bev said, and they stopped.

Bev was no leader. No Norman was. Perhaps that was their weakness, the reason why they had accomplished little. Conan, the nearest the Normans had to a leader, had been a fireman, doing a useful job, but only as an individual.

Bev, however, had at least one of the qualities of a leader. He wasn't afraid to take responsibility.

He started to go forward alone.

Conan caught up with him. 'Not you, Bev. Your potential is great – greater than anybody else's. But you've only been a Norman a very short time.'

Behind them, Sally tried to go after Bev and Jan tried to go after Conan. But they were held back.

After a long pause, Bev nodded. And it was Conan who walked on alone, naked, weaponless.

For a moment the peasants wavered. Then urged on by the Saxons behind, they rushed forward, flailing the air with their sticks. And seconds later they were flailing Conan. He went down.

Jan screamed. Conan was completely hidden by the mass of peasants, nearly all men, but with some women among them. The sticks still rose and fell.

The Norman-Saxons would have rushed forward, but Meredith held them back to a slow advance. The peasants saw them, retreated, and finally broke up. It was as if they suddenly realized, and only then, what they had done.

Conan lay still in the middle of the road. There was, strangely, no blood. But they knew, particularly the Normans who sense elan or its absence, that he was dead.

Conan Hersholt, who had said only a few minutes earlier:

'I can't kill peasants even if they kill me,' had proved his words. He died not even trying to defend himself.

One peasant only remained after the others had fled, to left or right, anywhere so long as it was away from both groups, away from both Normans and Saxons.

Seymour stared down at the body in sick horror. He had not managed to touch Conan. But he had had a stick, and it had been rising and falling like the others. His terror of Gardner and of what Gardner could do had made him do as he was told.

Still screaming, Jan ran forward. She dropped on her knees in the road, cradling Conan's head in her arms. Anastasia approached more slowly then stopped. Obviously she should check to make sure that Conan could not be revived. But it wasn't necessary.

'It should have been me,' said Bev.

'No,' Sally insisted. 'It should have been Conan.'

Seymour trudged away, dropping his stick. Nobody looked at him, for Meredith's Norman-Saxons and Gardner's Saxons now faced each other only a hundred yards apart.

Bev was uneasy about the guns. Conan had said: 'You don't have to worry about the guns.' But they had lost Conan.

There were now only Normans and Saxons in the street, plus Sally and Anastasia. But at every window they could see cautious, frightened, hopeful peasants.

The peasants, Bev sensed, were on their side. Rumors of the horror of Gardner's regime, speculation about the worse horrors that would follow his gaining total control, had spread among them.

Were the peasants out of the fight altogether? It seemed so. Stage one had been won by a human sacrifice.

More than that . . . From the sides of the broad street, five people joined them. Three of them threw off their clothes to declare themselves Normans. Two turned out to be Saxons.

It was cheering and significant that they had chosen to declare themselves at that precise moment – not afterwards when the battle was lost or won.

The Saxons stopped suddenly. Guns were levelled. Glenda, who had no gun, stood aside and watched.

Glenda, who had acted decisively throughout, was in fact confused.

It had seemed at first neither right nor wrong, but simply inevitable that the Normans and Saxons should fight. It would settle what had always been meant to be settled, which were meant to survive.

The fact that some Saxons joined the Normans had bothered her. That made it a totally different kind of battle. She was also concerned over the fact that the better Saxons had joined the other side and the worse were with Gardner.

Gardner was at the rear – not, she believed, because he was a coward but because he was grimly aware that some of his Saxons were scarcely more willing allies than the peasants had been.

Glenda it was who had to give the order. She would have preferred the Norman-Saxons to have guns. This was not because she wished to be shot, but because a certain feeling of fair play made her unhappy about firing on unarmed men and women.

However, it was entirely by their own choice that the other side were unarmed. They could have unearthed old weapons as Gardner had done.

She made her decision. 'Fire!' she ordered. And a moment later: 'Over their heads first.'

A dozen guns cracked. Nobody fell. The Normans stopped fifty yards away, but did not turn.

'Forward, and fire again,' said Glenda. 'Disable, don't kill.'

She was committed, but not fully committed yet. That would come if there was no surrender and the next order had to be: 'Shoot to kill.'

This time Bev did go forward. Something had to be settled. And by going forward he could be sure of drawing the Saxons' fire.

Two or three guns went off raggedly. Bev was not touched.

Perhaps, he thought, it was to be expected that any new talent should be self-preservative. Whatever he could do, it must logically work most strongly when he was in danger . . .

Sally ran from the main body to join him, and though at first he wanted her to go back, he slowly realized that possibly she could help him. Guns were being aimed at her too. He had an even stronger motive.

It happened. After a strange muffled crack, a Saxon with an ancient shotgun staggered back, holding his right eye. There was blood on his face. And two seconds later, as another gun went off, it jumped from the hand of the man who had held it, the barrel burst open.

The Saxons, a few of them, started throwing down their guns. One went off, the bullet shooting a Saxon in the chest.

It was no miracle. Anybody might have guessed that old guns loaded with old cartridges would blow up, misfire or jam. It was perhaps a little strange that they all apparently fired once, when they were pointed over the heads of the Norman-Saxons.

Bev remembered something Conan had once said: 'Coincidence? You'll get used to coincidence. If people have feelings, hunches, and act on them, you'll be surprised how many coincidences there are.'

At Bev's side Sally heard Gardner's voice from behind the Saxons, urging them on.

For a moment it seemed they wouldn't obey. Then they were on the move again. Without guns they were no worse off than their opponents, who never had any.

The two lines, which had never been particularly straight, miraculously levelled off. Bev and Sally did not go back to the ranks: the others closed around them.

Now dead straight, the two forces approached, more and more slowly as they got nearer.

And then, twenty yards apart, they stopped.

'Come on,' said Sally, dragging Bev by the arm.

'No.'

Anticlimax? If it was, it was the most potent anticlimax in history. The Normans were holding the Saxons back. Now Gardner was at the front with Glenda. Yet neither he nor Glenda moved forward, try as they might to exhort the others.

Everyone in the street and everyone watching the street was very much aware that the only casualty, the only Norman or Saxon killed, had been killed by peasants.

Fear? Bev asked himself. Were they instinctively, not knowing what they were doing, or how, making the Saxons afraid to make the next move? Any move?

Meredith said: 'Bev, it isn't enough. Defense isn't enough. You have to kill.'

'No.'

'We have to kill. It's not enough, I tell you. Maybe the Normans can shield themselves, but you can't shield the peasants too. If you let these Saxons go, they'll sidestep us and take over the peasants – send a thousand peasants against us instead of a hundred, kill ten of us instead of one.'

Bev murmured so that only Meredith could hear him: 'I can't kill any more than Conan could. It's something built into me. I have a vague idea of the thoughts and feelings that would make a man die, but I can't – '

'We can.' Meredith looked round significantly at the other Saxons in the group.

Then in full sight of them all, John Breaks felled Gardner with a stick. He pitched forward and lay still.

Glenda went for Breaks with nails and teeth.. Somebody pushed her back. Then the Saxons were fighting among themselves.

The Norman-Saxons moved back slightly, watching. Although Bev could not even try, with his mind, to kill Saxons, he had no objection whatever to watching Saxons kill themselves.

Glenda, after that quick instinctive reaction, stood aside. Long seconds passed. Gardner was somewhere underneath the milling mass, probably dead.

Slowly she walked over and joined the others. She didn't stand by Bev and Sally but with Meredith.

Meredith smiled.

But the battle, which for the moment had seemed to be over, was not. The Saxons not only fought themselves: berserk, they were now able to attack the Normans and the opposing Saxons, particularly the Saxons.

None had guns any more and only a few had sticks. And though many Normans were attacked, the attackers generally turned away from them after a few seconds.

They didn't turn away from Saxons whom they believed to be traitors.

Meredith went down. Sally and Anastasia dragged him away. With the crazed Saxons it was a case of out of sight, out of mind. They went for the nearest enemy . . . or friend.

Three of the women attacked Glenda. One of them had a knife. It was just about to be plunged into Glenda's heart when Bev, not knowing what he did, stabbed mentally at the woman.

She didn't fall, she didn't seem to be physically harmed. But she turned, stared at Bev, and then ran from the fray, the knife still clutched in her hand.

There were no lines any more. The Normans were not exactly retreating, they were guarding their own Saxons and letting Gardner's Saxons fight among themselves.

And as the battle wheeled, Jan, still kneeling over Conan was exposed. That was the word . . . exposed. Not so much because she was naked, with a dead Norman, but because she was alone, with nobody near her.

Three black-furred Saxons charged at her. At first she didn't even see them, which was strange, because every Norman in the wide street, every Saxon and even the peasants Sally and Anastasia were instantly aware of what was happening and sensed that it was important. Everything else stopped as they watched.

It was obvious to the Saxons as to everybody else that they had achieved virtually nothing throughout against the Normans. Those who were still in the fight with much the same feelings as they had had at the outset watched in hope – hope that this meant the turn of the tide. The fact that it was three big battle-crazed men against one small girl of sixteen was irrelevant. If Saxons could tear a Norman limb from limb, if the fact was demonstrated and proved beyond all doubt to all, then the battle was not over.

The battle might not yet have begun.

The last of the people in the street to know about the three bloodlusting men charging down on her, Jan looked up.

There was not time for her to think. She simply reacted, not in fear but in knowledge that these were three of the men who had killed Conan. It didn't matter to her that the fatal blows had been struck by peasants . . . but for these Saxons, the peasants would never have been there.

Everybody in the street *saw* what she did. A red glow formed about the three Saxons, contracting in on them and deepening in color as it did so. Yet this, clearly visible though it was and corroborated afterwards by scores of Normans, Saxons and peasants, was probably an illusion, a trick caused by mental awareness that something was happening, transformed into something thus interpreted by the eyes.

The Saxons' body hair went on fire (another illusion, since afterwards their fur was found to be undamaged). They stretched in every way they could – arms high, fingers splayed out, legs wide apart. And then they contracted, falling in heaps like three small chimpanzees.

But the display was not over. Jan was abruptly on her feet, stretching wildly as the Saxons had done. Nobody in the street had seen the Saxons from the front, but they saw Jan, since she was facing their way.

Every muscle of her hitherto soft body was stretched to the limit and beyond it. Not merely on the balls of her feet, she went literally on tiptoe, the toes themselves taking her weight. Her little breasts pointed to the sun, her ribs stood out as if there was no flesh on them, her midriff and abdomen became a yawning cavity in a pelvis that showed as if she had suddenly been disembowelled.

She could not survive it, of course. Although nobody was in no doubt then or later that it was something mental and not physical that burned her out, a human body could not be racked as hers was momentarily and be of any use afterwards.

She fell across Conan as if protecting him.

There was only a momentary pause in the mêlée. For a moment the Saxons were sobered by the demonstration that a Norman could kill without even touching the victim. But almost at once they were reassured by the fact that the Norman couldn't do it without dying too.

Then there was a sudden transformation. As if a siren had sounded from every direction peasants came running. Once more the struggling stopped. The worm had turned . . . had it turned on the Normans, or Saxons, or both?

They soon made it clear. They fell on the Saxons. Indeed,

the Normans found themselves protecting Gardner's Saxons as well as their own.

There were too many peasants. Gardner's Saxons ran.

On the street lay fourteen dead Saxons and two dead Normans, Conan and Jan. Arthur Gardner was not one of the Saxons.

Anastasia had her bag brought up and started tending the injured. Meredith, still dazed from the rough handling, helped her.

Sally said to Bev: 'We've got to go after Gardner. So long as he's alive, the whole thing could start again at any moment.'

Bev nodded. He looked around, and Sally shook her head. 'No. We don't need anybody. We'll go ourselves. There's two main places he might be – the factory and the house. You go to the factory. I'll go to the house.'

'Take half a dozen people with you.'

'Yes . . . Hurry. He's hurt. He must be.'

But when Bev had run off, she made no effort to recruit help. She got on her bicycle and set off. If Gardner made for the house, she'd reach it before him.

As she expected, there was no sign of life at Gardner's house. Gardner could not have reached it unless he used a car, and there was no car in the street.

She hid her bicycle behind a hedge and waited in the space between two houses.

And after just five minutes Gardner appeared, alone, still naked, limping.

It was only then that Sally realized she had no plan of action. It had been of the first importance to find Gardner, and she had done that. Physically she could handle him, but she could scarcely march him back to the center of town.

The fact that she had no plan worked out didn't bother her for long.

It was clear that Gardner had to die. There was no machinery, peasant or Norman or Saxon, to have him tried and sentenced, and it would take some time to set it up. Gardner would have some support. Far better to get rid of him quietly.

Could she kill him? Cold, no. She was no executioner. The

fact that she was a small girl of nineteen and he was a heavy man didn't enter into her calculations . . . what had to be done came first. *How* came later.

But if it were her or him, she could quite coolly decide that it had better be him. It therefore seemed to her quite reasonable to set up a situation in which it would be her or him.

So she stepped out, ran across the road and caught up with him as he reached the door and bent to grope for a concealed key.

'Right, Gardner,' she said. 'I've found you. Do I get the prize?'

'You do,' he said, and came up, not with a key in his hand but a small pistol.

Sally was not greatly perturbed. If anything could create a situation in which she would willingly and without compunction kill Arthur Gardner, it was his being armed and she unarmed. He wouldn't shoot her at once. He'd already proved that.

Carefully he bent again to the thick bush at the side of the door, still holding the gun on her, and this time he came up with the key.

He gave it to Sally. 'Open the door,' he said.

She went inside and he followed her. They went along the corridor and down the steps to the iron door. It was closed but not locked. Once they were inside, however, Gardner locked it and then did something rather surprising.

He put the big iron key in a metal press intended for more sinister uses. Still watching Sally closely, he spun the spindle until the jaws closed on the key, then gave the handle a heave. There was a sharp crack and when he released the press the key was broken.

'Nobody will ever get out of here,' he said significantly. 'Nobody.'

Sally had every intention of getting out, though she could not at the moment see how. There were no windows, the walls were solid and the door was even more solid. And the key was useless. It was the teeth which Gardner had broken.

'I'm glad you came, Sally,' said Gardner conversationally. 'I'm going to torture you to death. That will be very enjoyable. It could be for you too . . . Afterwards I'm going to torture myself to death. The supreme experience.'

As she made a slight move, the gun came up sharply.

'Don't,' he said. 'You know and I know that with no alternative facing you – incidentally, if your friends come now they won't force their way in here for a couple of hours at least, and that's more than enough time for me – the logical thing for you to do is to make me shoot you dead, clean and quick. Let me warn you, that if I have to shoot, I'll shoot you in the leg, the arm, the belly. And the rest of the program will proceed as planned.'

This was interesting. In his effort to shoot her so selectively, he might miss.

'I'd like to have you whip me, but I can't,' he said regretfully. And he went on talking in this vein, but Sally was no longer listening, for in the shadows behind the Iron Maiden she saw a man with a knife. She didn't know Seymour, but it was obvious that he hated Gardner and meant to kill him.

Many people, no doubt, had reason to hate Gardner.

Unwisely, perhaps, Seymour had let her see him. She might have screamed and given Gardner a chance to shoot him before he could get close. Sally, however, had too much presence of mind to do anything of the sort.

Seymour pantomimed instructions to keep Gardner occupied so that he could creep up on him. Gardner's unexpected possession of a gun had spoiled Seymour's plans as well as Sally's. Gardner only had to turn and he could drop Seymour long before Seymour could reach him.

In that case, Sally was quite confident she could get Gardner. She would probably not be able to prevent him shooting Seymour dead, but the momentary diversion would be enough to give her a chance to get the gun from Gardner.

She wondered fleetingly why Gardner's assumed special powers did not tell him that there was a man with a knife behind him.

Oddly enough, Gardner was talking about precognition. He was telling her about a vision he had had . . .

'You standing over me with a knife,' he said. 'That's why I let you go the first time. Later I realized it wasn't necessary. You're not dressed right. Either the vision is all accurate or it's not accurate at all.'

'How was I dressed?' Sally asked conversationally.

The picture flashed before Gardner's eyes again. Sally in short red pants and a red bra. Holding the red knife.

He grinned. 'If I told you, you might somehow be able to make it come true. No, I won't tell you. Anway, it's not what you're wearing now . . .'

Seymour was pantomiming even more desperately. Where he was, he could hide behind the huge Iron Maiden if Gardner turned. Once he left his cover, Gardner had an excellent chance of hearing his approach on the stone floor and turning in time to shoot him.

Sally took off her white shirt. She was watching Gardner's eyes, careful now not to look past him at Seymour. She expected to rivet Gardner's attention, and she did. But his expression didn't change when he saw her white bra. That, then, wasn't right either. He was not afraid of her in blue jeans and a white bra.

Seymour had made his move. He was out from cover now, creeping slowly, concentrating on not making a sound.

Sally reached behind her and unfastened the white bra. As Gardner stared at her naked breasts, she shook out the garment and started to put it on again.

It was reversible and the other side was red.

She saw sudden alarm in Gardner's eyes, his gun came up, and at the same moment Seymour stabbed him from behind. Refusing to rely on Seymour, Sally let the bra go and instinctively Gardner fired at it, missing it and missing Sally.

By this time Sally was on him, striking at the wrist which held the gun. Seymour slashed a second time, wildly, missed Gardner altogether and seared Sally across the knee. She felt a sharp pain but ignored it, fighting for the gun.

Seymour slashed again with the knife and missed. But in turning away Gardner exposed his back and this time Seymour could not miss. Gardner fell face down, trying as he fell to get in a shot at Seymour or Sally.

He could have had either of them and he knew that if he succeeded in killing Sally the vision could not come true and therefore this might not be death for himself . . . not yet. But with the gun on Sally and life ebbing from him, he suddenly said in a tone of surprise: 'Norman!' and shot Seymour.

Gardner was dead. Sally bent over Seymour and saw he was dying too. With the blood that came from his mouth came one word, the same as Gardner's last, but questioning: 'Norman?'

Puzzled, Seymour died.

Gardner's last vision was of a photograph he had in his possession, a photograph of Seymour's seven children. It was incredible that he had never realized before a man with seven children had to be a Saxon or a Norman – and Seymour was no Saxon.

So he killed Seymour instead of Sally.

Sally knew nothing of this and dismissed it with a shrug, since it was unlikely it would ever make sense to her. She picked up the bra and put it on, then took off her jeans, one leg of which was almost cut through by Seymour's wild swing. Her knee, however, had almost escaped. Despite the sharp pain, she found only a three-inch scratch which was scarcely bleeding.

The immediate problem was how to get out. There were plenty of powerful tools around, and an ordinary wooden door would have presented no problem. But the iron door . . .

Sally was practical. The heavy iron door was hung on massive hinges. They were inside, accessible. Huge iron eyes fitted on stout finger posts.

The very strength and massiveness of the hinges made them vulnerable. She ran a steel hawser from the rack to the finger posts and cranked the ancient mechanism of the rack. It was designed to break bodies, but it was an efficient and versatile machine. It broke the hinges one by one, and the iron door fell like Gardner's empire.

In red shorts and a red bra Sally, about to climb over the door to freedom, turned back, bent over Gardner and pulled out the knife. She didn't know why she did that. She could quite easily have left it where it was.

The Battle of Sherburn never made the papers, let alone the history books. Rumors spread in the district and to neighboring towns. But the general consensus of opinion was that nothing had happened beyond an untidy, riotous scuffle. Confrontation of Normans and Saxons was not mentioned. After all, peasants, Normans and Saxons were in it, apparently on both sides.

Anyway, within an hour every Norman and Saxon was clothed again.

All was back to normal.

In other towns, Normans and Saxons in high places saw to it that it didn't make the papers either.

But they were interested.

6

The two people in the old car which arrived in Sherburn, a man and a girl, both wore clean white overalls. The girl was driving.

The man said: 'I think we picked the right time.'

'You mean you picked it,' said the girl.

'They're together. Confused, needing a lead.'

'Well, that's something we can't give them. I thought we were here because they didn't need a lead?'

'Five days ago something happened, we're not sure what, and exactly what it was doesn't matter anyway. But there's been no advance. They don't know where to go. Look at these people.'

The people in London Road were as apathetic as ever, Sherburn had been shaken up, and as far as the peasants were concerned the big relief was that when it was all over nearly everybody was able to return to his rut. The factory was working again, under new management or no management, they didn't care, and it already seemed incredible that naked hairy people and naked hairless people had marched in this very street and a handful of them had died.

Since it was incredible, the peasants refused to believe it. The peasant motto was 'It's nothing to do with me.'

The bicycle girl was now better known in the town, almost famous. Her importance, however, was merely that whenever she appeared on her bicycle there were fresh food supplies including many commodities as rare as octopus had once been – and often regarded with similar suspicion. Cod, cod roe, herring, haddock, sprats, whiting. Mussels, prawns, shrimps. Veal, goose, duck, turkey. Mushrooms, tomatoes, paprika, cloves, garlic, red peppers, chillies. Oranges, bananas, lemons, grapefruit.

It was known that she was not producing exotic fruits and spices out of thin air, and that she was not selling at a loss. She was simply a successful business woman, something that had not been seen for a long time. When she was offered a ton of coffee if she would collect it herself from Tilbury Docks or Bristol, she accepted unhesitatingly, and one of her new army of helpers set off in a van. Then she would go round on her bicycle and do half a dozen deals with other suppliers.

Meredith Dundee, who had always been known and regarded with uneasy respect, had disappeared entirely from view. So had nearly all the known protagonists in the confrontation which was being studiously forgotten. Only Sally Wells and the woman doctor were out and about, busy, bringing sometimes welcome, usually unwelcome change.

Anastasia was trying to organize the health services of the town, with no great success so far. Once every doctor, dentist, nurse, midwife and druggist had been part of a great organization. When the money dried up, so did the network. Anastasia was trying to renew communications long severed and recreate services remembered only by the old.

She felt, obscurely, she owed it to Conan.

The two visitors saw neither Sally on her bicycle nor Anastasia in her old two-seater car, and seeing only peasants they saw little evidence of any change in the town.

The man said: 'It's a small thing, but aren't they moving around a little faster?'

'Scared somebody's behind them?' the girl retorted.

'Yes, that maybe. It's not always a bad thing to be looking over your shoulder.'

'Where now?'

'Carry on. I think this is the right road. A big house, with a swimming pool.'

'A swimming pool? With real water?'

'I think there's real water.'

It was not difficult to find Meredith Dundee's house. They got out of the car. A mere glance at the blank, well-kept but forbidding frontage made them turn without comment to the path that led round the side of the house.

The three gates with their system of latches and springs interested them both. They did not constitute either a puzzle to be solved or a test of strength. They were merely a mild challenge: *Do you really want to get through?*

'Clever,' said the girl. 'I bet it works too. A Saxon idea, not a Norman.'

The man nodded.

There were half a dozen people round the pool. The man and the girl, pausing in the dark shadow of the house, were not noticed, the others being in bright sunlight.

Not one of them was naked. On the other hand, not one of them was fully clothed, except Anastasia, and she and Sally were the only two who did not immediately proclaim themselves Norman or Saxon. Meredith, Bev, Joan and Glenda were in swimsuits of various shapes and sizes. Meredith and Glenda were obvious Saxons, Glenda's golden fur already beginning to identify her. Bev and Joan were so preternaturally hairless that their nature was clear at a glance. Sally, in shorts, could have been a Norman . . . but the man and girl, both of whom had good eyes, spotted the faint down on her brown legs which set her apart from Joan Bush.

'The peasants don't *want* to know,' Meredith insisted. 'They want an easy, uncomplicated life. They'll work harder for a better standard of life if they're given the chance. They slightly resent us but they don't want to fight us.'

'They don't want their noses rubbed in it,' Glenda said, agreeing.

Sally said firmlv: 'They've got to face facts. As I faced them. As Anastasia and I faced them.'

'No,' said Anastasia. 'You may mean that as a compliment, Sally, but it doesn't happen to be true. I didn't face the facts. I quietly acknowledged them – maybe I had to, with a Norman brother – and that's all I did.'

'You're facing them now.'

'Reluctantly. Meredith's right. Every peasant in Sherburn knows now there are two new super-races – '

'We don't call ourselves super-races,' said Bev quietly.

'No, but we do. We're the peasants. We know it, we can't

do anything about it, we don't particularly want to do anything about it, but we don't have to like it.'

Sally was obstinate as ever. 'I don't see it. Bev's better than me at some things, I'm better than he is at others. I don't feel I have to crawl away into a corner and die because I'm a peasant – '

'You're not a peasant,' said the man in overalls.

By this time two of the group round the pool had noticed them, naturally enough the two Normans. Joan, who had not previously been able to identify a clothed Saxon just by looking at her, found she now could. And Bev was interested by the obvious fact – obvious to him – that the two were Norman and Saxon and as close as any two people could be.

'I'm a peasant,' said Sally firmly, 'and I don't give a damn.'

'You're not a peasant, because you don't give a damn,' the man retorted.

He and the girl stepped forward. The Normans knew who they were – strangers, envoys. The Saxons could guess.

The man started to take off his overalls. He seemed to wear nothing underneath, and his pale body was totally hairless. The girl was covered in fine reddish fur.

'It's not necessary,' said Bev. 'We know.'

'You didn't go naked during the trouble?' said the girl. 'It usually happens.'

'During the trouble, yes. Not since. The peasants don't like it.'

'They never do,' said the girl, zipping up her overalls.

'You're from London?' said Bev.

'It doesn't really matter where we're from. We've come to help you, if we can.'

'I don't think,' said Sally, 'we need any help.'

The man took that up. 'If you don't know you're not a peasant, you do.'

'All right. Tell me how.'

'Nature makes a lot of mistakes. One of them was *homo sapiens.* He was a good idea, but essentially unstable. Bound to die out in the end. Not survival material. True, he lasted for a few million years, but that's nothing to the galaxy. Once he started reaching out, from about the nineteenth century, he hadn't long to go.'

'The wars were a lesson,' said the girl. 'The world wars, I mean. And surprisingly, *homo sap* nearly learned it. He learned enough to stop fighting big destructive wars. But he didn't learn what to put in their place. And what not to put.'

Meredith Dundee said: 'Pollution. Industrial, political, social, ideological anarchy. The simple philosophy *I want.*'

'Yes,' the girl agreed. 'Plus permissiveness. Funny how even near the end *homo sap* didn't realize permissiveness was suicide. Abandonment of law. Abdication of responsibility.'

'So we got the peasants,' said Bev thoughtfully.

'Then nature made another mistake,' said the girl, the Saxon girl. 'The Saxons.'

Meredith wasn't surprised or angry that she described Saxons as a mistake. 'We were first, then?' he asked.

'We think so. It doesn't matter. Saxons, on the whole, are bound to do more harm than good. Too many are unstable. We get locked up, and that's the one thing we can't stand. And every now and then, a really dangerous Saxon is born. Have you got one?'

'We had,' said Meredith significantly.

The man said: 'After that, nature made yet another mistake – the Normans.'

'My brother was a Norman,' said Anastasia. 'I don't accept that he was a mistake. He was extremely stable, and his whole life was in the public good – '

'And he's dead,' said the man brutally. 'At about twenty-five, eh? No, we're all mistakes. Normans as much as Saxons. We may be more stable, but . . . '

He looked at Bev, sensing something. 'You may amount to something now,' he admitted. 'How much did you amount to three months ago?'

'Nothing,' Bev admitted.

'Oh, nature had to do something,' the man went on. 'The old girl was trying. And failing. Then at last she really hit on something.'

He looked straight at Sally. 'The real new people. We haven't got a name for them yet. Mainly because they steadfastly refuse to accept any special name that anybody tries to give them. They're very new. Not one is as old as thirty. There seem to be very few of them, but in fact there are far more than we know, far more than we'll ever know, because they insist they're peasants.'

They were all interested now, except Sally, who didn't like this sort of talk.

'Define them,' Meredith suggested. 'We know about Normans and Saxons. What characterizes these . . . other people?'

The man shrugged. 'I just got here. You all know this girl Sally. Define her and you've got your answer.'

'Sally's my wife,' said Bev. 'I know her, yet not as well as I'd know a Norman – any Norman. I don't mind. I like it that way. All the same, you tell me – what are these other people like?'

It was the girl, the Saxon girl, who answered. 'Anti-Norman and anti-Saxon. That doesn't mean necessarily in conflict with both. It means flat refusal to be like Normans or like Saxons. Saxons can't influence them, Normans can't even sense them, right? You, good-looking Norman, love this girl and yet unless she wants you to you can't even tell she's in the next room, right? They've all got that, a mind shield you can call it if you like.'

'We think,' the man supplemented, 'it's deliberate. The new people *won't* be Saxons and they *won't* be Normans. A peasant doesn't have a mind shield. We think that nobody could have anything that acts like a mind shield without some of the mental abilities of a Norman. But the new people won't use them. They don't need them. They get on without them. For the number one characteristic of the new people is that every one of them is a success.'

Sally was taken aback, for all the time she had been insisting she was a peasant she had also been claiming to be practical . . . which meant exactly the same as what the Norman meant.

Just about the only thing in which she had ever failed totally was trying to keep David alive. But she had known all along she was going to fail in that. For the rest, she always expected to succeed. It was nothing to do with having the golden touch – she always had to work for her successes. And she always achieved them.

She had never feared Vince Hobley or Arthur Gardner or any of the other Saxons or Normans or peasants or situations. And she was a little ashamed to have to face the realization that this was not because she had courage but because she knew she would win.

The two strangers, to the astonishment of all of them, turned to go.

'That's all?' said Meredith incredulously.

'Oh, we'll be in touch. But the main thing you've got to do is obvious, isn't it?'

'Not exactly.'

'You're lucky. You've got one of the new people, and she'll live another seventy years. Do exactly what you were going to do, but put her in charge. Oh, not officially. Leave your apparent Saxon boss in charge with the usual Normans behind him . . . but let Sally do the real deciding. Let her run you as she runs her . . . ?'

'Shops,' Bev supplied, smiling.

The girl, already at the corner of the house, looked back. 'In five years you won't know the place,' she said.

THE END

THE SHIP WHO SANG by ANNE McCAFFREY

The brain was perfect, the tiny, crippled body useless. So technology rescued the brain and put it in an environment that conditioned it to live in a different kind of body – a spaceship. Here the human mind, more subtle, infinitely more complex than any computer ever devised, could be linked to the massive and delicate strengths, the total recall, and the incredible speeds of space. But the brain behind the ship was entirely feminine – a complex, loving, strong, weak, gentle, savage – a personality, all-woman, called Helva . . .

0 552 10163 X – 80p

RESTOREE by ANNE McCAFFREY

There was a sudden stench of a dead sea creature . . .
There was the horror of a huge black shape closing over her . . .
There was nothing . . .
Then there were pieces of memory . . . isolated fragments that were so horrible her mind refused to accept them . . . intense heat and shivering cold . . . excruciating pain . . . dismembered pieces of the human body . . . sawn bones and searing screams . . . And when she awoke she found she was in a world that was not earth, and with a face and body that were not her face and body. She had become a Restoree . . .

0 552 10161 3 – 75p

LOGAN'S RUN by WILLIAM F. NOLAN and GEORGE CLAYTON JOHNSON

It was a nightmare society – a world of the 'cubs' – rebel hipsters drugged to a point of frenzy . . . of a vast underwater city gradually collapsing under the pressures of the sea . . . of an ice hell in polar regions where criminals were sent to survive if they could . . . of a desert inhabited by psychotic savages.

It was a world where there was little beauty and no peace . . . where man, condemned to a short lifespan, fought against his own terror and dreamed of Sanctuary . . .

0 552 10123 0 – 50p

THE DOORS OF HIS FACE, THE LAMPS OF HIS MOUTH by ROGER ZELAZNY

A collection of fifteen stories of man in the future, ranging in time from a few decades to a few millenia into the future, in setting from the solar system to deepest space. The prize-winning title story is the highly imaginative and very believable tale of a fishing expedition for an enormous sea monster under the oceans of the planet Venus; the rest of the collection maintains the high standard thus set, with tales of a rebellious preacher's son finding a different religion on Mars, of an expedition to an electrically-haunted mountain where a girl is discovered in hibernation state awaiting the discovery of a cure for her fatal disease, and of man's penchant for aggrandizement. All display the style, wit, imagination which have made Roger Zelazny one of the most highly praised writers of science fiction today.

0 552 10021 8 – 50p

THIS IS THE WAY THE WORLD BEGINS by J. T. McINTOSH

From the holiday planet of Paradiso one could go on many exciting tours and excursions – Mars, Venus, the Moon, even the most distant and alien worlds were accessible to the inquisitive holidaymaker, courtesy of Starways Inc. – the giant combine which owned Paradiso and over half the galaxy.

But of all Starways illustrious trips, there was really only one which interested Ram Burrell – the one which Starways seemed to actually discourage people from taking . . . the trip to planet Earth.

0 552 10432 9 – 70p

WILL–O–THE–WISP by THOMAS BURNETT SWANN

Will-o-the-wisp – the light that danced across the Devon moors – enticing the good puritan people to death and devilment . . . For up on the tors dwelt the infamous Gubbings who crucified their victims, murdered and bewitched . . .

Were they really warlocks, or were they creatures of fantasy from another time, another planet?

Robert Herrick, poet, vicar and pagan, the golden giant with a lusty heart, dared to brave the moors and challenge the ancient myth . . .

0 552 10358 6 – 60p